Adrian Mole:
The Wilderness Years

DOSTOYEVSKY · NOTES FROM THE UNDERGROUND

ENGLISH LOVE POEMS

COLIN WILSON — THE OUTSIDER

Adrian Mole:
The Wilderness Years

SUE TOWNSEND

LONDON NEW YORK SYDNEY TORONTO

*The line drawings in the text
are by Caroline Holden*

This edition published 1993
by BCA
by arrangement with Methuen London

CN 2483

Typeset by Falcon Graphic Art Ltd
Wallington, Surrey
Printed in England by Clays Ltd, St Ives plc

To my sisters, Barbara and Kate

'What's gone and what's past help
Should be past grief.'

William Shakespeare
The Winter's Tale

Tuesday January 1st 1991

I start the year with a throbbing head and shaking limbs, owing
to the excessive amounts of alcohol I was forced to drink at my
mother's party last night.

I was quite happy sitting on a dining chair, watching the
dancing and sipping on a low-calorie soft drink, but my mother
kept shouting at me: 'Join in, fishface,' and wouldn't rest until
I'd consumed a glass and a half of Lambrusco.

As she slopped the wine into a plastic glass for me, I had
a close look at her. Her lips were surrounded by short lines,
like numerous river beds running into a scarlet lake; her hair
was red and glossy almost until it reached her scalp and then
a grey layer revealed the truth: her neck was saggy, her cleavage
wrinkled and her belly protruded from the little black dress (*very*
little) she wore. The poor woman is forty-seven, twenty-three
years older than her second husband. I know for a fact that he,
Martin Muffet, has *never* seen her without make-up. Her pillow
slips are a disgrace; they are covered in pan-stick and mascara.

It wasn't long before I found myself on the improvised dance
floor in my mother's lounge, dancing to 'The Birdie Song', in
a line with Pandora, the love of my life; Pandora's new lover,
Professor Jack Cavendish; Martin Muffet, my boyish stepfather;
Ivan and Tania, Pandora's bohemian parents; and other inebri-
ated friends and relations of my mother's. As the song reared
to its climax, I caught sight of myself in the mirror above the
fireplace. I was flapping my arms and grinning like a lunatic.
I stopped immediately and went back to the dining chair. Bert
Baxter, who was a hundred last year, was doing some clumsy
wheelchair dancing, which caused a few casualties; my left ankle
is still bruised and swollen, thanks to his carelessness. Also I have
a large beetroot stain on the front of my new white shirt, caused
by him flinging one of his beetroot sandwiches across the room
under the misapprehension that it was a party popper. But the

poor old git is almost certain to die this year – he's had his tele-gram from the Queen – so I won't charge him for the specialist dry cleaning that my shirt is almost certain to require.

I have been looking after Bert Baxter for over ten years now, going back from Oxford to visit him, buying his vile cigarettes, cutting his horrible toenails, etc. When will it end?

My father gate-crashed the party at 11.30. His excuse was that he wanted to speak urgently to my grandma. She is very deaf now, so he was forced to shout above the music. 'Mum, I can't find the spirit level.'

What a pathetic excuse! Who would be using a spirit level on New Year's Eve, apart from an emergency plumber? It was a pitiful request from a lonely, forty-nine-year-old divorcee, whose navy blue mid-eighties suit needed cleaning and whose brown moccasins needed throwing away. He'd done the best he could with his remaining hair, but it wasn't enough.

'Any idea where the spirit level is?' insisted my father, looking towards the drinks table. Then he added, 'I'm laying some paving slabs.'

I laughed out loud at this obvious lie.

My grandma looked bewildered and went back into the kitchen to microwave the sausage rolls and my mother graciously invited her ex-husband to join the party. In no time at all, he had whipped his jacket off and was frugging on the dance floor with my eight-year-old sister Rosie. I found my father's style of dancing acutely embarrassing to watch (his role model is still Mick Jagger); so I went upstairs to change my shirt. On the way, I passed Pandora and Bluebeard Cavendish in a passionate embrace half inside the airing cupboard. He's old enough to be her father.

Pandora has been mine since I was thirteen years old and I fell in love with her treacle-coloured hair. She is simply playing hard to get. She only married Julian Twyselton-Fife to make me jealous. There can be no other possible reason. Julian is a bisexual semi-aristocrat who occasionally wears a monocle. He strains after eccentricity but it continues to elude him. He is a deeply ordinary man with an upper-class accent. He's not even good-looking. He looks like a horse on two legs. And as for her affair with Cavendish, a man who dresses like a tramp, the mind boggles.

Pandora was looking particularly beautiful in a red off-the-shoulder dress, from which her breasts kept threatening to escape. Nobody would have guessed from looking at her that she was now Dr Pandora Braithwaite, fluent in Russian, Serbo-Croat and various other little-used languages. She looked more like one of those supermodels that prowl the catwalks than a Doctor of Philosophy. She certainly added glamour to the party: unlike her parents, who were dressed as usual in their fifties beatnik style – polo necks and corduroy. No wonder they were both sweating heavily as they danced to Chuck Berry.

Pandora smiled at me as she tucked her left breast back inside her dress, and I was pierced to the heart. I truly love her. I am prepared to wait until she comes to her senses and realises that there is only one man in the world for her, and that is *me*. That is the reason I followed her to Oxford and took up temporary residence in her box room. I have now been there for a year and a half. The more she is exposed to my presence, the sooner she will appreciate my qualities. I have suffered daily humiliations, watching her with her husband and her lovers, but I will reap the benefits later when she is the proud mother of our six children and I am a famous author.

As the clock struck twelve, everyone joined hands and sang 'Auld Lang Syne'. I looked around, at Pandora; at Cavendish; at my mother; at my father; at my stepfather; at my grandma; at Pandora's parents, Ivan and Tania Braithwaite; and at the dog. Tears filled my eyes. I am nearly twenty-four years of age, I thought, and what have I done with my life? And, as the singing died away, I answered myself – nothing, Mole, nothing.

Pandora wanted to spend the first night of the New Year in Leicester at her parents' house with Cavendish, but at 12.30 a.m. I reminded her that she and her aged lover had promised to give me a lift back to Oxford. I said, 'I am on duty in eight hours' time at the Department of the Environment. At 8.30 sharp.'

She said, 'For Christ's sake, can't you have one poxy day off without permission? Do you have to kow-tow to that little commissar Brown?'

I replied, with dignity, I hope, 'Pandora, some of us keep our word, unlike you, who on Thursday the second of June 1983 promised that you would marry me as soon as you had finished your "A" levels.'

Pandora laughed, spilling the neat whisky in her glass. 'I was sixteen years old,' she said. 'You're living in a bloody time warp.'

I ignored the insult. 'Will you drive me to Oxford as you promised?' I snapped, dabbing at the whisky droplets on her dress with a paper serviette covered in reindeer.

Pandora shouted across the room to Cavendish, who was engaged in conversation with Grandma about the dog's lack of appetite: 'Jack! Adrian's insisting on that lift back to Oxford!'

Bluebeard rolled his eyes and looked at his watch. 'Have I got time for one more drink, Adrian?' he asked.

'Yes, but only mineral water. You're driving, aren't you?' I said.

He rolled his eyes again and picked up a bottle of Perrier. My father came across and he and Cavendish reminisced about the Good Old Days, when they could drink ten pints in the pub and get in the car and drive off 'without having the law on your back'.

It was 2 a.m. when we finally left my mother's house. Then we had to call at the Braithwaites' house to collect Pandora's overnight bag. I sat in the back of Cavendish's Volvo and listened to their banal conversation. Pandora calls him 'Hunky' and Cavendish calls her 'Monkey'.

I woke up on the outskirts of Oxford to hear her whisper: 'So, what did you think of the festivities at Maison Mole, Hunky?'

And to hear him reply: 'As you promised, Monkey, delightfully vulgar. I enjoyed myself enormously.' They both turned to look at me, so I feigned sleep.

I began to think about my sister Rosie, who is, in my view, totally spoilt. The *Girls' World* model hairdressing head she had demanded for Christmas had stood neglected on the lounge window sill since Boxing Day, looking out onto the equally neglected garden. Its retractable blond hair was hopelessly tangled and its face was smeared with garish cosmetics. Rosie was dancing earlier with Ivan Braithwaite in a manner totally unsuited to an eight-year-old. They looked like Lolita and Humbert Humbert.

Nabokov, fellow author, you should have been alive on that day. It would have shocked even you to see Rosie Mole pouting in her black miniskirt, pink tights and purple cropped top!

* * *

I have decided to keep a full journal, in the hope that my life will perhaps seem more interesting when it is written down. It is certainly not interesting to actually live my life. It is tedious beyond belief.

Wednesday January 2nd

I was ten minutes late for work this morning. The exhaust pipe fell off the bus. Mr Brown was entirely unsympathetic. He said, 'You should get yourself a bicycle, Mole.' I pointed out that I have had three bicycles stolen in eighteen months. I can no longer afford to supply the criminals of Oxford with ecologically sound transport.

Brown snapped, 'Then *walk*, Mole. Get up earlier and *walk*.'

I went into my cubicle and shut the door. There was a message on my desk informing me that a colony of newts had been discovered in Newport Pagnell. Their habitat is in the middle of the projected new ring road. I rang the Environmental Office at the Department of Transport and warned a certain Peter Peterson that work on the ring road could be subject to delay.

'But that's bloody ludicrous,' said Peterson. 'It would cost us hundreds of thousands of pounds to re-route that road, and all to save a few slimy reptiles.'

That is also my own private point of view of newts. I'm sick of them. But I am paid to champion their right to survive (in public at least), so I gave Peterson my standard newt conservation lecture (and pointed out that newts are amphibians, not reptiles). I spent the rest of the morning writing up the Newport Pagnell case.

At lunchtime I left the Department of the Environment and went to collect my blazer from the dry cleaners. I had forgotten to take my ticket. (It was at home, being used as a bookmark inside Colin Wilson's *The Outsider*. Mr Wilson is Leicester-born, like me.)

The woman at the cleaners refused to hand over my blazer, even though I pointed to it hanging on the rack! She said, 'That blazer has got a British Legion badge on it. You're too young to be in the British Legion.'

An undergraduate behind me sniggered.

Enraged, I said to the woman, 'You are obviously proud of your powers of detection. Perhaps you should write an *Inspector Morse* episode for the television.' But my wit was lost on the pedant.

The undergraduate pushed forward and handed her a stinking duvet, requesting the four-hour service.

I had no choice but to go home and collect the ticket, go back to the cleaners, and then run with the blazer, encased in plastic, slung over my shoulder, all the way back to the office. I have got a blind date tonight and the blazer is all I've got to wear.

My last blind date ended prematurely when Ms Sandra Snape (non-smoking, twenty-five-year-old, vegetarian: dark hair, brown eyes, five foot six, not unattractive) left Burger King in a hurry, claiming she'd left the kettle on the stove. I am now convinced, however, that the kettle was an excuse. When I returned home that night, I discovered that the hem was down at the back on my army greatcoat. Women don't like a scruff.

I was twenty-five minutes late getting back to work. Brown was waiting for me in my cubicle. He was brandishing my Newport Pagnell newt figures. Apparently I had made a mistake in my projection of live newt births for 1992. Instead of 1,200, I had put down 120,000. An easy mistake to make.

'A hundred and twenty thousand newts in 1992, eh, Mole?' sneered Brown. 'The good citizens of Newport Pagnell will be positively inundated with amphibia.'

He gave me an official warning about my time-keeping and ordered me to water my cactus. He then went to his own office, taking my paperwork with him. If I lose my job, I am done for.

11.30 p.m. My blind date did not turn up. I waited two hours, ten minutes in the Burger King in the town centre. Thank you, Ms Tracy Winkler (quiet blonde, twenty-seven, non-smoker, cats and country walks)! That is the last time I write to a box number in the *Oxford Mail*. From now on, I will only use the personal column of the *London Review of Books*.

Thursday   January 3rd

I have the most terrible problems with my sex life. It all

boils down to the fact that I *have* no sex life. At least not with another person.

I lay awake last night, asking myself why? Why? Why? Am I grotesque, dirty, repellent? No, I am none of these things. Am I normal-looking, clean, pleasant? Yes, I am all of these things. So what am I doing wrong? Why can't I get an average-looking young woman into my bed?

Do I exude an obnoxious odour smelled by everyone else but me? If so, I hope to God somebody will tell me and I can seek medical help from a gland specialist.

* * *

At 3 a.m. this morning my sleep was disturbed by the sound of a violent altercation. This in itself is not unusual, because this house provides a home for many people, most of them noisy, drunken undergraduates, who sit up all night debating the qualities of various brands of beer. I went downstairs in my pyjamas and was just in time to see Tariq, the Iraqi student who lives in the basement, being led away by a gang of criminal-looking men.

Tariq shouted, 'Adrian, save me!' I said to one of the men, 'Let him go or I will call the police.'

A man with a broken nose said, 'We *are* the police, sir. Your friend is being expelled from the country, orders of the Home Office.'

Pandora came to the top of the basement stairs. She was wearing very little, having just left her bed. She said in her most imperious manner: 'Why is Mr Aziz being expelled?'

'Because,' said the thuggish one, 'Mr Aziz's presence is not conducive to the public good, for reasons of national security. Ain't you 'eard there's a war on?' he added, ogling Pandora's satin nightshirt, through which the outline of her nipples was clearly visible.

Tariq shouted, 'I am a student at Brasenose College and a member of the Young Conservatives: I am not interested in politics!'

There was nothing we could do to help him, so Pandora and I went back to bed. Not the same bed though, worse luck.

* * *

At nine o'clock the next morning, I rang the landlord, Eric Hardwell, on his car phone and asked if I could move into the now vacant basement flat. I am sick of living in Pandora's box room. Hardwell was in a bad mood because he was stuck in traffic, but he agreed, providing I can give him a £1000 deposit, three months' rent in advance (£1200), a banker's reference and a solicitor's letter stating that I will not burn candles, use a chip pan, or breed bull terrier dogs in the basement.

I shall have to stay here in the box room. I need to use my chip pan on a daily basis.

Lenin was right: all landlords *are* bastards.

Somebody who looked like Tariq was on *Newts At Ten*; he was waving from the steps of an aeroplane which was bound for the Gulf. I waved back in case it was him.

Correction: I meant, of course, to write *News At Ten*.

Friday   January 4th

Woke up at 5 a.m. and was unable to get back to sleep. My brain insisted on recalling all my past humiliations. One by one they passed in front of me: the bullying I endured from Barry Kent until my grandma put a stop to it; the day at Skegness when my father broke the news to me and my mother that his illegitimate son, Brett, had been born to his lover, Stick Insect; the black day when my mother ran away to Sheffield for a short-lived affair with Mr Lucas, our smarmy neighbour; the day I learned that I had failed 'A' level Biology for the third time; the day Pandora married a bisexual man.

Then, after the humiliations came the *faux pas*, a relentless march: the time I sniffed glue and got a model aeroplane stuck to my nose; the day my sister, Rosie, was born and I couldn't remove my hand from the spaghetti jar where the five pound note for the taxi fare to the maternity hospital was kept; the time I wrote to Mr John Tydeman at the BBC and addressed him as 'Johnny'.

The procession of *faux pas* was followed by a parade of bouts of moral cowardice: the time I crossed the road to avoid my father because he was wearing a red pom-pom hat; my craven behaviour when my mother was stricken with a menopausal temper tantrum in the Leicester market place – I should not have walked away and hidden behind that flower stall; the day I had a jealous fit, destroyed the complimentary tickets for Barry Kent's first professional gig on the poetry circuit and blamed the dog; my desertion of Sharon Bott when she announced she was pregnant.

I despise myself. I deserve my unhappiness. I am truly a loathsome person.

I was relieved when my travelling alarm clock roused me from my gloomy reverie and told me that it was 6.30 a.m. and time to get up.

Nipples by A. Mole
Like raspberries
taken from the freezer
Inviting tongue and lips
but warning not to bite
Not yet
soon
But not yet

I am on flexitime and had agreed to start work at 7.30 a.m., but somehow, although I left my box room at 7 a.m., I didn't arrive at work until 8 a.m. A journey of half a mile took me an hour. Where did I go? What did I do? Did I have a blackout on the way? Was I mugged and left unconscious? Am I, even as I write, suffering from memory loss?

Pandora is constantly telling me that I am in urgent need of psychiatric help. Perhaps she is right. I feel as though I am going mad; that my life is a film and that I am a mere spectator.

Saturday   January 5th

Julian, Pandora's upper-crust husband, has returned from his Christmas sojourn in the country with his parents. He shuddered when he walked through the front door of the flat.

'God!' he said. 'The pantry of Twyselton Manor is bigger than this bloody hole.'

'Then why come back, sweetie?' said Pandora, his so-called wife.

'Because, *ma femme*, my parents, poor, deluded creatures, are paying mucho spondulicks to keep me here at Oxford, studying Chinese.' He laughed his neighing horse's laugh. (And he's certainly got the teeth for it.)

'But you haven't been to a lecture for over a year,' said Dr Braithwaite (12 'O's, 5 'A's, B.A. Hons. and D.Phil.).

'But my lecturers are all such boring little men.'

'It's such a waste, husband,' said Pandora. 'You're the cleverest man in Oxford *and* the laziest. If you're not careful, you'll end up in Parliament.'

After Julian had thrown his battered pigskin luggage into his room, he returned to the kitchen, where Pandora was chopping leeks and I was exercising my new sink plunger. 'So, darlings, what's new?' he said, lighting one of his vile Russian cigarettes.

Pandora said, 'I'm in love with Jack Cavendish, and he's in love with me. Isn't it absolutely marvellous?' She grinned ecstatically and chopped at the leeks with renewed fervour.

'Cavendish?' puzzled Julian. 'Isn't he that grey-haired old linguistics fart who can't keep his plonker in his pants?'

Pandora's eyes flashed dangerously. 'He's sworn to me that from now on his lifestyle will be strictly non-polygynous,' she said.

She stretched up to replace the knife on its magnetic rack and her cropped tee shirt rode up, revealing her delicate midriff. I thrust the plunger viciously into the greasy contents of the sink, imagining that Cavendish's head was on the end of the wooden stick, instead of the black rubber suction pad.

Julian neighed knowingly. 'Cavendish doesn't know the meaning of the word "non-polygynous". He's a notorious womaniser.'

'*Was*,' insisted Pandora, adding, 'and *of course* he knows the meaning of the word "non-polygynous": he is a professor of Linguistics.'

I left the plunger floating in the sink and went to my box room, took my *Condensed Oxford Dictionary* from its shelf and, with the aid of the magnifying glass, looked up the word 'non-polygynous'. I then uttered a loud, cynical laugh. Loud enough, I hoped, to be heard in the kitchen.

Sunday January 6th

Woke at 3 a.m. and lay awake remembering the time when Pandora and I nearly went All the Way. I love her still. I intend to be her second husband. And what's more, she will take my name. She will be known as 'Mrs Adrian Albert Mole' in private.

> *On Seeing Pandora's Midriff*
> The glorious shoreline from ribcage
> To pelvis
> Like an inlet
> A bay
> A safe haven
> I want to navigate
> To explore
> To take readings from the stars
> To carefully trace my fingers
> Along the shoreline
> And eventually to guide my ship, my destroyer, my
>   pleasure craft
> Into and beyond your harbour

6.00 p.m. Sink still blocked. Worked for three hours in the kitchen, adding vowels to the first half of my experimental novel *Lo! The Flat Hills of My Homeland*, which was originally written with consonants only. It is eighteen months since I sent it to Sir Gordon Giles, Prince Charles's agent, and he sent it back, suggesting I put in the vowels.

Lo! The Flat Hills of My Homeland explores late twentieth-century man and his dilemma, focusing on a 'New Man' living in a provincial city in England.

The treatment is broadly Lawrentian, with a touch of Dostoievskian darkness and a tinge of Hardyesque lyricism.

I predict that one day it will be a G.C.S.E. set book.

I was driven out of the kitchen by the arrival of that wrinkled-up ashtray on legs, Cavendish, who had been invited to Sunday lunch. He hadn't been in the flat two minutes before he was pulling a cork out of a bottle and helping himself to glasses out of the cupboard. He then sat on *my* recently vacated chair at the kitchen table and began to talk absolute gibberish about the Gulf War, predicting that it would be over within months. I predict that it will be America's second Vietnam.

Julian came into the kitchen, wearing his silk pyjamas and carrying a copy of *Hello!*

'Julian,' said Pandora, 'meet my lover, Jack Cavendish.' She turned to Cavendish and said, 'Jack, this is Julian Twyselton-Fife, my husband.' Pandora's husband and Pandora's lover shook hands.

I turned away in disgust. I'm as liberal and civilised as the next person. In fact, in some circles I'm regarded as quite an advanced thinker, but even I shuddered at the utter depravity that this introduction signified.

I left the flat to get some air. When I returned from my walk around the Outer Ring Road two hours later, Cavendish was still there, telling tedious anecdotes about his numerous children and his three ex-wives. I microwaved my Sunday lunch and took it into my box room. I spent the rest of the evening listening to laughter in the next room. Woke at 2 a.m. and was unable to get back to sleep. Filled two pages of A4 devising tortures for Cavendish. Not the actions of a rational man.

Tortures for Cavendish
1) Chain him to the wall with a glass of water *just* beyond his grasp.
2) Chain him naked to a wall while a bevy of beautiful girls walk by, cruelly mocking his flaccid *and* aroused penis.
3) Force him to sit in a room with Ivan Braithwaite, while Ivan talks about the finer details of the Labour Party's Constitution, with particular reference to Clause Four. (This is true torture, as I can bear witness.)
4) Show him a video of Pandora getting married to me. She radiant in white, me in top hat and tails, putting two gloved fingers up at Cavendish.

Let the punishment fit the crime.

Monday January 7th

Started my beard today.

Some of the Newport Pagnell newts have crossed the road. I telephoned Peterson at the Department of Transport, to inform him. There has obviously been a split in the community. I expect a female newt is at the bottom of it: *cherchez la femme*.

Wednesday January 9th

For the first time in my entire life I haven't got a single spot, pustule or pimple. I pointed out to Pandora over breakfast that my complexion was flawless, but she paused in applying her mascara, looked at me coldly, and said, 'You need a shave.'

Spent ten minutes at the sink with the plunger before going to work, but to no avail. Pandora said, 'We'll have to get a proper man in.'

Does Pandora realise the impact the above words, so apparently casually uttered, have had on me? She has disenfranchised me from my gender! She has cut my poor, useless balls off!

Thursday January 10th

Brown has advised me to shave. I refused. I may have to seek the advice of the Civil and Public Service Union.

Friday January 11th

Applied to join the C.P.S.U.

Pandora found Cavendish's A4 torture list. She has made an appointment for me to see her friend Leonora De Witt, who is a psychotherapist. I agreed reluctantly. On the one hand, I am terrified of my unconscious and what it will reveal about me. On the other, I am looking forward to talking about myself non-stop for an hour without interruption, hesitation or repetition.

Saturday January 12th

Pandora's most recent ex-lover, Rocky (Big Boy) Livingstone, came round to the flat today, asking for the return of his mini sound-system. At six foot three and fifteen stone of finely-honed muscle, Rocky is a 'proper' man, if ever I saw one. Pandora was out, meeting some of Cavendish's children at the Randolph Hotel. So, in her absence, I gave the sound-system to him. Since he and Pandora split up, Rocky has opened new gyms in Kettering, Newmarket and Ashby-de-la-Zouch. He and his new girl friend, Carly Pick, are still happy.

Rocky said, 'Carly's a real star, Aidy. I respect the lady, y'know.' I told Rocky about Professor Cavendish. He was disgusted.

He said, 'That Pandora is a *user*. Just 'cos she's clever, she finks she's . . .' He flailed about for the right word and finished, 'clever'.

Before he went he unblocked the sink. I was very grateful. I was getting sick of washing the pots in the bathroom hand basin. None of the saucepans would fit under the taps.

I went to the window and watched him drive away. Carly Pick had both her arms around his neck.

Sunday   January 13th

The Gulf War deadline expires on the 15th, at midnight. What will I do if I am called up to fight for my country? Will I cover myself with honour, or will I wet myself with fear on hearing the sound of enemy gunfire?

Monday   January 14th

Went to Sainsbury's and stocked up with tins of beans, candles, Jaffa cakes, household matches, torch batteries, Paracetamol, multivitamins, Ry-King and tins of corned beef and put them in the cupboard in my box room. Should the war spread over here, I will be well prepared. The others in the flat will just have to take their chance. I predict panic buying on a scale never seen before in this country. There will be fighting in the aisles of the supermarkets.

Appointment with Leonora De Witt on Friday 25th of this month at 6 p.m.

Tuesday January 15th

Midnight. We are at war with Iraq. I phoned my mother in Leicester and told her to keep the dog in. It is twelve years old and reacts badly to unexpected noises. She laughed and said, 'Are you going mad?' I said, 'Probably,' and put the phone down.

Wednesday January 16th

Bought sixteen bottles of Highland Spring water, in case water supply is cut off owing to bombardment by Iraqi airforce. It took me four trips from the Spar shop on the corner to the flat, but I feel more secure knowing I will not go thirsty during the coming *Blitzkrieg*.

Brown has not mentioned my beard for some days now. He is preoccupied with the effect that 'Operation Desert Storm' will have on the desert wildlife. I said, 'I'm afraid I regard Iraqi wildlife as being on the side of the enemy. I'm more worried about my dog, at home in Leicester.'

'Ever the parochial, Mole,' said Brown, in a lip-curling manner. I was quite insulted. Brown reads nothing, apart from journals on wildlife, whereas I have read most of the Russian Greats and am about to embark on *War and Peace*. Hardly parochial, Brown!

Thursday January 17th

I have hired a portable colour television, so I can watch the Gulf War in bed.

Friday January 18th

The spokesperson for the U.S.A. military is a man who calls himself 'Colon Powell'. Every time I see him, I think of intestines and the lower bowel. It detracts from the gravity of the War.

Saturday January 19th

Bert Baxter rang me up at the office today. (I will kill whoever gave him the number.) He wanted to know 'when you

and my favourite gal are comin' to see me?' His 'favourite gal'
is Pandora. Why doesn't Bert just *die* like other pensioners? His
quality of life can't be up to much. He is nothing but a burden
to others (me).

He was entirely ungrateful when I dug a grave for his dog,
Sabre, last year, though I challenge anyone to dig a neater hole
in compacted soil with a rusty garden trowel. If I'd had a decent
spade at my disposal, then, *naturellement*, the grave would have
been neater. The truth is that I hated and feared Sabre. The
day the wretched Alsatian died was a day of rejoicing for me. No
more smelling its noxious breath. No more forcing Bob Martin's
conditioning tablets between its horrible vicious teeth.

Bert burbled on about the war for a while, and then asked
me if I had heard my old enemy Barry Kent on *Stop the Week*
this morning. Apparently, Kent was publicising his first novel,
Dork's Diary. I am now utterly convinced there cannot be a God.
It was me that encouraged Kent to write poetry, and now I find
out that the ex-skinhead, frozen peabrain has written a novel,
and got it published!!!

Pandora told me this evening that Kent made Ned Sherrin,
A. S. Byatt, Jonathan Miller and Victoria Mather laugh almost
continuously. Apparently the phone lines at the BBC were jammed with listeners asking when *Dork's Diary* will be published
(Monday). This is absolutely and totally the last straw. My sanity
hangs by a fragile thread.

Sunday   January 20th

I was passing Waterstone's bookshop when I saw what appeared
to be Barry Kent standing in the window. I lifted my hand in
greeting and said, 'Hello, Baz,' then realised that the smirking
skinhead was only a cardboard cut-out. Copies of *Dork's Diary*
filled the window. I'm not ashamed to say that curses sprang
from my lips.

As I flicked through the pages of the slim volume, my
eye was caught not only by the many obscenities with which
the book is littered, but by the name – 'Aiden Vole' – given
to one of the characters. This 'Aiden Vole' is obsessed with
matters anal. He is jingoistic, deeply conservative and a failure
with women. 'Aiden Vole' is an outrageous caricature of me,

without a doubt. I have been slandered. I shall see my solicitor in the morning. I shall instruct him or her (I haven't actually got a solicitor yet) to demand hundreds of thousands of pounds in damages. I couldn't bring myself actually to buy a copy of the book. Why should I add to Kent's royalties? But I noticed as I left the shop that Kent is giving a reading from *Dork's Diary* on Tuesday evening at 7 p.m. I will be in the audience. Kent will leave Waterstone's a broken man when I have finished with him.

Monday   January 21st

The Cubicle, D.O.E.

Just listened to Kent on *Start the Week* on my portable radio. He has certainly extended his vocabulary. Melvyn Bragg said that the Aiden Vole character was 'wonderfully funny' and asked if he was based on anybody real. Kent laughed and said, 'You're a writer, Melv; you know what it's like. Vole is an amalgam of fact and fantasy. Vole stands for everything I hate most in this country, after the new five-pence piece, that is.' The other guests – Ken Follett, Roy Hattersley, Brenda Maddox and Edward Pearce – laughed like drains.

Spent the rest of the morning looking through the Yellow Pages for a solicitor with a name I can trust. Chose and rang 'Churchman, Churchman, Churchman and Luther'. I am seeing a Mr Luther at 11.30 a.m. on Thursday. I am supposed to be visiting the Newport Pagnell newts on Thursday morning with Brown, but he will just have to face them alone. My reputation and my future as a serious novelist are at stake.

Alfred Wainwright, who wrote guides to the fells of the Lake District, died today. I once used Mr Wainwright's maps when I attempted to do the 'coast to coast' walk with the 'Off the Streets' Youth Club. Unfortunately, I developed hypothermia within half an hour of leaving the Youth Hostel at Grimsby and my record-breaking attempt had to be abandoned.

Tuesday   January 22nd

Review of *Dork's Diary* in *The Guardian*:

'A coruscating account of *fin de siècle* provincial life.
Brilliant. Dark. Hilarious. Buy it!' Robert Elms

Box Room 10 p.m.
Couldn't get in to see Kent; all the tickets were sold. Tried
to speak to him as he entered the shop, but couldn't get near
to him. He was surrounded by press and publicity people. He
was wearing sunglasses. In January.

Wednesday   January 23rd

Beard coming along nicely. Two spots on left shoulder blade.
A slight pain in anus, but otherwise I am in superb physical
condition.

Read long interview in the *Independent* with Barry Kent. He
told lies from start to finish. He even lied about the reason for
his being sent to prison, claiming he was sentenced to eighteen
months for various acts of violence, when I know very well that
he got four months for criminal damage to a privet hedge. I have
faxed the *Independent*, putting the record straight. It gave me no
pleasure to do this, but without the Truth we are no better than
dogs. Truth is the most important thing in my life. Without Truth
we are lost.

Thursday   January 24th

Lied on the phone to Brown this morning and told him that I
could not visit the Newport Pagnell newt habitat on account of
a severe migraine. Brown ranted on about how he had 'never
taken a day off work in twenty-two years'. He went on to brag
that he had 'even passed several massive kidney stones into the
lavatory at work'. Perhaps that explains why the lavatory basin
is cracked.

I was late for my appointment with Mr Luther, the solicitor,
though I left the flat in plenty of time – another time warp or
memory-loss – a mystery, anyway. As I told Luther (in great
detail) about Kent's slander of me, I noticed him yawning several
times. I expect he was up late; he looks the dissolute type. He
was wearing braces covered in pictures of Marilyn Monroe.

Eventually he raised his hand and said, 'Enough, I've heard

enough,' in an irritable sort of way. Then he leaned across his desk and said, 'Are you vastly rich?'

'No,' I replied, 'not vastly.'

He then asked, 'Are you desperately poor?'

'Not desperately. That's why I . . .'

Luther interrupted before I could finish my sentence, 'Because unless you are vastly rich, or desperately poor, you can't possibly afford to go to court. You don't qualify for Legal Aid and you can't afford to pay a barrister a thousand pounds a day, can you?'

'*A thousand pounds a day?*' I said, absolutely aghast.

Luther smiled, revealing a gold back molar.

I remembered my grandma's advice, 'Never trust a man with a gold tooth.' I thanked Mr Luther politely but coldly and left his office. So much for English justice. It is the worst in the world. As I passed the waiting room, I noticed a copy of *Dork's Diary* on the coffee table, next to copies of *Amnesty* and *The Republican*.

Got home to find a note from Leonora De Witt informing me that she is unable to keep our appointment tomorrow. Why? Is she having her hair done? Is double-glazing being installed in her consulting room? Have her parents been found dead in bed? Am I so unimportant that my time is a mere plaything to Ms De Witt? She suggested a new appointment: Thursday 31st January at 5 p.m. I left a message on her Ansafone, agreeing to the new arrangement, but announcing my displeasure.

Saturday   January 26th

I was awake all last night, watching 'Operation Desert Storm'. I feel it's the least I can do – after all, it is costing H.M. Government thirty million pounds a day to keep Kuwait a democracy.

Sunday   January 27th

According to the *Observer* today, Kuwait is not and has never been a democracy. It is ruled by the Kuwaiti Royal Family.

Bluebeard laughed when I told him. 'It's all to do with *oil*, Adrian,' he said. 'Do you think the Yanks would be in there if Kuwait's main product was *turnips*?'

Pandora bent down and kissed the back of his withered

neck. How she could allow her young, vibrant flesh to come into contact with his ancient, wrinkled skin, I'll never know. I had to go into the bathroom and take deep breaths and control the urge to vomit. Why slobber over *him* when she could have *me*?

My mother rang at 4 p.m. I could hear my young stepfather, Martin Muffet, hammering in the background. 'Martin's putting some shelves up for my knick-knacks,' she shouted over the row. Then she asked me if I had read the extracts from *Dork's Diary* in the *Observer*. I was able to answer truthfully. 'No,' I said. 'You should,' said my mother. 'It's totally brilliant. When you next see Baz, will you ask him for a free copy, signed to Pauline and Martin?'

I said, 'It is highly unlikely that I will see Kent. I do not move in the same illustrious circles as him.'

'Which illustrious circles *do* you move in, then?' asked my mother.

'None,' I answered truthfully. Then I put the phone down and went to bed and pulled the duvet over my head.

Monday   January 28th

Britain's Jo Durie and Jeremy Bates won the mixed doubles in Melbourne. This surely points to a renaissance in British tennis.

> *Pandora's Little Pussy*
> I love her little Pussy
> Her coat is so warm
> But if I should stroke her
> She'll call the police and identify me in
> A line-up
> And do me some harm

Wednesday   January 30th

Shocked to hear on Radio Four that King Olav the Fifth of Norway was buried today. His contribution to the continuing success of the Norwegian leather industry is something that is little appreciated by the vast majority of the Great British Public. Prince Charles was England's graveside representative.

Borrowed *Scenes from Provincial Life* by William Cooper from the library. I only had time to choose one book, because a 'suspicious package' was found in the Romantic Fiction section and the library was evacuated.

Sink blocked again. Plunged for the duration of *The Archers*, but to no avail.

Thursday   January 31st

I didn't arrive at the consulting room on Thames Street until 5.15 p.m. Leonora De Witt was not pleased.

'I'll have to charge you for the full hour, Mr Mole,' she said, seating herself in an armchair which was covered in old bits of carpet. 'Where would you like to sit?' she asked. There were many chairs in the room. I chose a dining chair which was standing against a wall.

When I was seated, I said, 'I was under the impression that our sessions were to be under the auspices of the National Health Service.'

'Then you were gravely mistaken,' said Ms De Witt. 'I charge thirty pounds an hour – under the auspices of the private enterprise system.'

'*Thirty pounds an hour!* How many sessions will I need?' I asked.

She explained that she couldn't possibly predict, that she knew nothing about me. That it depended on the cause of my unhappiness.

'How do you feel at the moment?' she asked.

'Apart from a slight headache, I feel fine,' I replied.

'What are you doing with your hands?' she said quietly.

'Wringing them,' I replied.

'What is that on your brow?' she asked.

'Sweat,' I answered, taking out my handkerchief.

'Are your buttocks clenched, Mr Mole?' she pressed.

'I suppose they are,' I said.

'Now answer my first question again, please. How do you feel at this moment?'

Her large brown eyes locked into mine. I couldn't avert my gaze.

'I feel totally miserable,' I said. 'And I lied about the headache.'

She talked at length about the *Gestalt* technique. She explained that it was possible to teach me 'coping mechanisms'. Apart from Pandora, she is probably the loveliest woman I have ever spoken to. I found it hard to take my eyes off her black-stockinged feet, which were slipped into black suede shoes with high heels. Was she wearing tights or stockings?

'So, Mr Mole, do you think we can work together?' she said.

She looked at her watch and stood up. Her hair looked like a midnight river pouring down her back. I eagerly affirmed that I would like to see her once a week. Then I gave her thirty pounds and left.

Friday   February 1st

Just returned from Newport Pagnell. My nerves are shot to pieces. Brown drove like a man possessed. At no time did he exceed the speed limit, but he drove onto the kerb, scraped against hedgerows and on the motorway section of our journey he left only a six-inch gap between our fragile Ford Escort and the monolithic juggernaut in front of us.

'It saves precious fuel if you can stay in the lorry's slipstream,' he said by way of explanation. The man is an environmental fanatic. He spent last Christmas Day classifying seaweed at Dungeness. I rest my case. Thank God for the weekend. Or *le weekend*, as our fellow Europeans say.

Saturday   February 2nd

Viscount Althorp, Princess Diana's brother, has confessed to his thin wife and the rest of the world that he had an affair in Paris. Prince Charles and Princess Diana must have been horrified to find out that there was an adulterer in the family. He should be stripped of his title immediately. The Royal Family and their close connections should be above such brutish instincts. The country looks to them to set the moral standard.

Had bath, shampooed beard, cut fingernails and toenails. Put hot oil on hair to nourish it and give it shine and the outward illusion of health.

11.45 p.m. Bert Baxter has just telephoned. He sounded pathetic. Pandora was out and in a moment of weakness I agreed to go and visit him in Leicester tomorrow. Wrote a note to Pandora, left it on her pillow.

> Pandora,
> Baxter rang in considerable distress, something about killing himself – I intend to visit him tomorrow. He intimated to me that he wished to see you too. I plan to rise at 8.30 to catch the train, or, should you wish to accompany me, my alternative *modus operandi* will be to rise at nine and be driven by you in your motor car, thus arriving in Leicester at approximately 11 a.m. Would you please inform me of your decision by the method of slipping a note under my door? Please do not disturb me tonight with the sounds of your wild love-making. The walls of my box room are very thin and I am sick of sleeping with my Sony Walkman on.
>
> Adrian

Sunday   February 3rd

At 2.10 a.m., Pandora burst into my box room and hurled abuse at me. She flung my note to her into my face and screamed, 'You pompous *nerd*, you pathetic *dork*! "*Modus operandi*"! "Be driven by you in your motor car"! I want you out of this box room and out of my life, *tomorrow*!'

Bluebeard came in and led her away and I lay in bed and listened to them murmuring together in the kitchen. What brought on such an unprovoked outburst?

At 3.30 a.m. they went into Pandora's bedroom. At 3.45 a.m. I put Dire Straits into my Sony and turned the volume up to full.

Didn't wake until midday. 'Phoned Bert and said I was unable to visit him owing to being awake all night with intestinal pains. I could tell Bert didn't believe me. He said, 'You're a bleedin' liar. I've just spoken to my gal Pandora. She rang me on her car phone. She looked in your room before she set out for Leicester and she said you were sleepin' like a newborn.'

'Why didn't she wake me then?' I asked.

' 'Cos she 'ates the bleedin' sight of you,' said the diplomatic one.

Monday   February 4th

Inexplicably late for work by twenty-three minutes. Brown was practically frothing at the mouth. Also accused me of stealing postage stamps. He said, 'Every penny is needed by the D.O.E. if our wildlife is to be preserved.' As if! Are the badgers and foxes and tadpoles and lousy, stinking newts going to pop their clogs because I, Adrian Mole, made use of two second-class postage stamps paid for out of my taxes in the first place? No, Brown. I don't think so.

Tuesday   February 5th

Pandora still in Leicester. Trimmed beard around mouth. Swallowed clippings. One lodged at back of throat; annoying.

Wednesday   February 6th

Brown came into my cubicle today and demanded to see my 'A' level certificates! He had heard on the office grapevine that I had failed 'A' level Biology three times. The only person in Oxford – apart from Pandora – who knows about my triple failure is Megan Harris, Brown's secretary. I confessed to her whilst in a drunken and emotional state at the D.O.E. Christmas Party last year. She alone knows that my job as a Scientific Officer Grade One was granted to me under false pretences. Has Megan blabbed? I must know.

I told Leonora De Witt my family history tonight. It's a tragic story of rejection and alienation, but Leonora simply sat and picked balls of fluff from her sweater, which drew my attention to the shape of her comely breasts. It was obvious that she was not wearing a bra. I wanted to leave my chair and sink my head into her bosom. I went into some detail about my parents' deviant behaviour, but the only time she showed obvious interest was when I mentioned my dead grandfather, Albert Mole, whom I have to thank for my middle name.

'Did you see his dead body?' she asked.

'No,' I replied. 'The Co-op undertaker had screwed the coffin lid down and nobody could find the screwdriver at Grandma's house, so . . .'

'Continue,' ordered Leonora. So I did. Through fat, hot tears. I told about my feeling of exclusion from 'normal' life; of how I long to join my fellow human beings, to share their sorrows, their joys, their sing-songs in pubs.

Leonora said, 'People sing awful songs in pubs. Why do you feel a need to join in singing those mawkish lyrics and banal tunes?'

'I stood outside such pubs as a child,' I said. 'Everybody sounded so happy.'

Then the alarm went off on her watch and it was time to cough up thirty quid and leave.

On my way home I went into a pub and had a drink. I also initiated a conversation about the weather with an old man. There was no singing, so I went home.

Thursday February 7th

I asked Megan outright this morning. I approached her in the corridor as she was being scalded by the Autovent tea/coffee/ox-tail soup machine. She admitted that she had let it 'slip out' that I was totally unqualified for my position. Then she swore me to secrecy and informed me that she and Brown have been having an affair since 1977! Brown and the lovely Megan! Why do women throw themselves at worn-out old gits like Brown and Cavendish, and ignore young, virile, bearded men like me? It defies logic.

Megan was eager to talk about her affair with Brown. Apparently he had sworn to leave Mrs Brown in 1980, but has not yet done so. I feel sorry for Mrs Brown every time she comes into the office. It is not her fault that she looks like she does. Some women have got good dress sense and some women haven't. Mrs Brown obviously does not know that pop socks should only be worn under trousers or long skirts. Also, somebody should tell her that warts can be cured nowadays.

Friday February 8th

Pandora is back in Oxford, but not speaking to me much, apart from the bare facts that Bert is no longer suicidal. She bought him a kitten and also installed a cat flap in his back door. Brown asked me again for my Biology 'A' level certificate. I looked at him enigmatically and said, 'I think you'll find that Megan has the information you require.' God, blackmail is an ugly word. I hope Brown doesn't force me to use it.

I have thrown my condom away. It had exceeded its 'best before' date.

Monday   February 11th

Megan came into my cubicle today, sobbing. Apparently Brown forgot her birthday, which was yesterday. Alack, alas! It looks as if I am cast into the role of Megan's only confidant. I put my arms around her and kissed her. She felt lovely and soft and squashy. She pulled away quite soon, however, and said 'Your beard is scratchy and horrible.'

But was my beard the *real* reason?

Does my breath stink? Does my body stink?

Who can I trust to tell me the truth?

I can certainly see what Brown sees in Megan, but I will never in a billion years see what she sees in him. He is forty-two, thin, and wears atrocious clothes from 'Man at C&A'. Megan says he is good in bed. Who is she trying to kid? Good at what in bed? Doing jigsaws? Sleeping? Perhaps she means that he is unselfish with the duvet? If Brown is good in bed, then I am a tractor wheel.

Tuesday   February 12th

Tried to visit newt habitat in Northamptonshire, but 'wrong kind of snow' caused Class 317 engine to fail. Was forced to sit in freezing carriage whilst buffet bar attendant gave out continuous announcements in annoying adenoidal voice. Was pleased when buffet car ran out of all supplies and closed. Got back to Oxford at 10.30 p.m., to find message from Megan. Rang her to find out that she and Brown had had a row; their affair is over. I was distraught. This means I no longer have a hold over Brown. It could signal the end of my career with the D.O.E.

Wednesday   February 13th

Brown/Megan affair is on again. Apparently Brown cycled round to Megan's flat in the early hours, after telling Mrs Brown he was going bat-watching. Their reconciliation was very passionate.

I cannot imagine anything in the world more distasteful than seeing Brown in a state of orgasmic pleasure. Apart from *being* with Brown in a state of orgasmic pleasure.

Bought new condom – spearmint flavoured.

Also bought bunch of bananas. Megan says they are very good for those, like me, who suffer from an irritable bowel.

Thursday   February 14th

Valentine's Day card from my mother as usual. Megan in tears again. Brown forgot. Bought economy box of tissues at lunchtime for Megan's sole use. I can't afford to keep wasting Kleenex on her. Bluebeard has sent Pandora a disgracefully extravagant bouquet (it is disgusting when people are starving), and at seven o'clock this evening he called with champagne, an Art Nouveau brooch and a pair of satin pyjamas. Then, as if that wasn't enough, he took her out for dinner in a hired car with uniformed driver! Most unacademic behaviour.

Cavendish behaves more like a pools winner than a professor of Linguistics at an ancient seat of learning.

Left to myself, I ate a simple meal of bread, tuna and cucumber and went to bed early. I am reading *English Love Poems*, edited by John Betjeman. Valentine's Day is a ridiculous charade, the ignorant masses are manipulated by the greetings card companies into forking out millions – and for what? For the illusion of being loved.

Friday   February 15th

A Valentine's Day card! Signed 'A Secret Admirer'! I sang in my bath. I walked to work without touching the pavement! Who is she? The signature told me that she is educated and uses a felt-tip pen, like me.

Leonora had her hair pinned up today; she was wearing silver earrings so long that they brushed her slim shoulders.

She was wearing a scooped-neck black top. A bra strap was visible. Black lace. She occasionally pushed it back inside her top. Every time she did so her sparkling bracelet fell down her arms towards her elbow. I am not in love with Leonora De Witt. But I am obsessed with her. She invades my dreams. She made me talk to an empty chair and pretend that it was my mother. I told the chair that it drank too much and wore its skirts too short.

Saturday February 16th

I finally took my library books back today: *A Single Man* by Christopher Isherwood, *English Love Poems* by John Betjeman, *Scenes from Provincial Life* by William Cooper and *Notes from the Underground* by Dostoievsky. I owed seven pounds, eighty pence in fines. My least favourite librarian was on duty at the desk. I don't know her name, but she is the Welsh one with the extroverted spectacles.

After I'd written out my cheque and handed it to her, she said, 'Do you have a cheque card?'

'Yes,' I replied. 'But it's at home.'

'Then I'm afraid I cannot accept this cheque,' she said.

'But you know me,' I said. 'I've been coming here once a week for eighteen months.'

'I'm afraid that I don't recognise you at all,' she said and handed me my cheque back.

'This beard is quite recent,' I said coldly. 'Perhaps you could try to visualise my face without it.'

'I don't have time for visualisation,' she said. 'Not since the cuts.'

I showed her a small photograph of myself that I carry in my wallet. It was taken pre-beard.

'No,' she said, after giving it a cursory glance. 'I don't recognise that man.'

'But that man is *me!*' I shouted. A queue of people had built up behind me and they were listening avidly to the exchange. The librarian's spectacles flashed in anger.

'I have been doing the job of three people since the cuts began,' she said. 'And you are making my job even more difficult. Please go home and find your cheque card.'

'It is now 5.25 p.m. and the library closes in five minutes,' I said. 'Even Superman couldn't fly back in time to
pay the fines, choose four books and leave before the doors
close.'

Somebody behind me in the queue muttered, 'Get a bleedin'
move on, Superman.'

So I said to the spectacled one, 'I'll be back tomorrow.'

'Oh no you won't,' she said, with a tiny smile. 'Due to
the cuts this library doesn't open again until Wednesday.'

On my way home I railed internally against a government
that is depriving me of new reading matter. Pandora has forbidden me to touch her books ever since I left a Jaffa cake
inside her Folio Society edition of *Nicholas Nickleby*; Julian's
books are in Chinese and I'm finding the last hundred pages
of *War and Peace* heavy going. There is no way I can afford
to buy a new book. Even a paperback costs at least a
fiver.

I have to cough up thirty pounds a week for Leonora. I have
even had to cut down on my consumption of bananas. I am
down to one a day.

I have been forced to read my old diaries. Some of the
entries are incredibly perceptive. And the poems have stood the
test of time.

Sunday   February 17th

Pandora spoke to me today. She said, 'I want you to leave.
You stultify me. We had a childhood romance, but we are both
adults now: we have grown in different directions and the
time has come to part.' Then she added, cruelly, I thought,
'And that bloody beard makes you look absolutely ridiculous.
For God's sake, shave it off.' I went to bed shattered. Read
page 977 of *War and Peace*, then lay awake staring into the
darkness.

Monday   February 18th

I looked into the newsagent's on my way to work. I saw the
following advertisement, written in a reasonably educated hand,
on a Conqueror postcard:

Large sunny room to let – in family house. Fire sign
preferred. Use of W machine/dryer. £75pw inclusive to
N/S male professional. Ring Mrs Hedge.

I rang Mrs Hedge as soon as I got to my cubicle. She asked
for my date of birth. I told her it was April 2nd, which excited
the response, 'Aries, good. I'm Sagittarius.'

I went to see her at 7 p.m. and inspected the room. 'It's
not very sunny,' I said.

She said, 'No, but would you expect it to be on an evening
in February?'

I like the cut of her jib. She is oldish (thirty-five to thirty-seven,
I would guess), but has not got a bad figure, although it's hard to
tell with the clothes women wear nowadays. Her hair is lovely;
treacle-coloured, like Pandora's used to be before she started
mucking about with Colour-Glo. She was wearing quite a bit
of make-up and her mascara had smudged. I hope this is not a
sign of sluttishness. She was recently divorced and needs to let
the room in order to continue paying the mortgage. Apparently
the Building Society (my own, coincidentally) has turned nasty.

She invited me to test the bed. I did so and had a sudden
vision of myself and Mrs Hedge engaging in vigorous sexual
intercourse. I said aloud, 'I'm sorry.'

Naturally Mrs Hedge was completely in the dark as to the
reason for my apology and said, ' "Sorry"? Does that mean you
don't like the bed?'

'No, no,' I gibbered. 'I love you; I mean, I love the bed.'

I was concerned that I hadn't made a good impression, so I
rang Mrs Hedge when I got home (in an effort to impress her)
and informed her that I was a writer; would the scratching of
my pen in the small hours bother her?

'Not at all,' she replied. 'I am visited by the Muse myself
in the night occasionally.'

You can't walk on the pavement in Oxford without bumping
into a published or unpublished writer. It's no wonder that the
owner of the stationery shop where I buy my supplies goes to the
Canary Islands twice a year and drives a Mercedes. (He drives a
Mercedes in *Oxford*, not the Canary Islands, though of course it is
perfectly feasible that he has the use of a Mercedes *in* the Canary
Islands as well. But I doubt, given the comparative infrequency

of his visits, if he actually *owns* a Mercedes in the Canary Islands though I suppose it could be leased.) I don't know why I felt the need to explain the Canary Islands/Mercedes confusion. I suppose it may be another example of what Leonora calls my 'childish pedantry'.

Tuesday   February 19th

My mother rang in a panic at 11.00 p.m., to ask if Martin Muffet, my young stepfather, had turned up at the flat. Quite frankly, I laughed out loud. Why would Muffet want to visit *me*? He knows I disapprove of my mother's foolhardy second marriage. Apart from the age difference (which is as wide as the mouth of the Amazon), they are physically and mentally incompatible.

Muffet is a six foot six bag of bones, who thinks the Queen works hard and that Paddy Ashdown is incapable of telling a lie. My mother is five foot five and squeezes herself into clothes two sizes too small for her and thinks that Britain should be a republic and that our first president should be Ken Livingstone, the well-known newt lover. On my last visit, I noticed that young Mr Muffet was far less attentive to my mother than of late. I expect he is regretting his mad rush into matrimony.

My mother said, 'He went to London this morning, to visit the Lloyd's building for his Engineering course.'

My mother's grasp of the geographical layout of the British Isles has always been minimal. I informed her of the distance from the Lloyd's building in the City of London to that of my box room in Oxford.

She said in a pathetic voice, 'I thought he might have popped in on his way back to Leicester.'

She phoned back at 2 a.m. Muffet was trapped in an underground train in a tunnel for six hours, or so he said.

Thursday   February 21st

This time Leonora invited me to imagine that the chair was my father. She gave me an African stick and I beat the chair until I lay limp and exhausted and physically unable to lift the stick again.

'He's not a bad bloke, my dad,' I said, 'I don't know why I went so berserk.'

Leonora said, 'Don't talk to me, talk to him. Talk to the chair. The chair is your father.'

I felt stupid addressing the empty chair again, but I wanted to please Leonora, so I forced myself to look the upholstery in the eye and said, 'Why didn't you buy me an anglepoise lamp when I was revising for my G.C.S.E.s?'

Leonora said, 'Good, good, take it further, Adrian.'

'I hate your Country and Western cassettes,' I said.

'No,' Leonora whispered. 'Deeper, darker, an earlier memory.'

'I remember when I was three,' I said. 'You came into the bedroom, yanked my dummy out of my mouth and said, "*Real* boys don't need a dummy."'

I then grabbed the stick from where it was lying on the floor and once again began to beat the chair. Dust flew.

Leonora said, 'Good, good. How do you *feel?*'

I said, 'I feel terrible. I've wrenched my shoulder beating that chair.'

'No, no,' she said, irritably. 'How do you feel *inside?*'

I cottoned on.

'Oh, at peace with myself,' I lied. I got up, gave my thera-peutic dominatrix the thirty quid and left. I needed to buy some Nurofen before the late-night chemist closed. I was in agony with my shoulder.

Friday   February 22nd

Another split in the Newport Pagnell newts. There are now three separate habitats. Something fishy is happening in the newt world. Brown is phoning newt experts worldwide, droning on about this phenomenon.

Mrs Hedge has interviewed other potential tenants, but has chosen me! I was racked all night by erotic dreams, concern-ing me, Brown, Megan and Mrs Hedge. I am ashamed, but what can I do? I can't control my subconscious, can I? I was forced to go to the launderette, though it is not my usual day.

Saturday   February 23rd

Norman Schwarzkopf was on television tonight, pointing a stick at an incomprehensible map. Why he was dressed in army camouflage is a mystery to me:

- a) there are no trees in the desert
- b) there were no trees in the briefing room
- c) he is obviously too important to go anywhere near the enemy; he could go around dressed like Coco the Clown and still not be shot at

Tuesday   February 26th

Visited Mrs Hedge today, to finalise arrangements for renting the room and to discuss our tenancy agreement. She had a picture of the charred head of an Iraqi soldier who was found dead in a vehicle held against her fridge by a Mickey Mouse magnet. I averted my eyes and asked her for a drink of water.

Wednesday   February 27th

Yesterday evening I informed Pandora that I am moving out of the flat at the weekend. I had hoped that she would fall on my neck and beg me to stay, but she didn't. At 1 a.m. I was woken by the sound of a champagne cork popping, glasses clinking and wild, unrestrained laughter from Pandora, Cavendish and Julian. The Infernal Triangle.

Thursday   February 28th

Leonora did most of the talking tonight. She told me that I expect too much of myself, that I have impossibly high standards. She told me to be kind to myself and made me draw up a list of ten things I enjoy doing. Every time I banish a negative thought about myself, I am allowed to treat myself.

   She asked if I can afford the occasional self-indulgence. I confessed that I have savings in the Market Harborough Building Society. She gave me a piece of paper and a child's crayon and told me to write down ten treats.

Treats
1) Reading novels
2) Writing novels
3) Sexual intercourse
4) Looking at women
5) Buying stationery
6) Eating bananas
7) Crab paste sandwiches
8) Watching boxing on television
9) Listening to Tchaikovsky
10) Walking in the countryside

I asked Leonora what her treats were.

She said in a husky low voice, 'We're not here to talk about me.' Then she smiled and showed her beautifully white teeth and said, 'We have a few things in common, Adrian.'

I felt a throb of sexual desire surge through me.

'I too like to watch the boxing on television,' she said. 'I'm a Bruno fan.'

Friday   March 1st

At breakfast this morning, I asked Cavendish if he would help me to move my things to Mrs Hedge's. He has got a big Volvo estate. He said, 'Can't think of anything I'd rather do, Aidy.' He offered to move me immediately, but I said, 'Tomorrow morning will do. Some of us have to *work*.'

He laughed and said, 'So you think teaching Linguistics is a soft option, do you, Aidy?'

I said, 'Yes, as a matter of fact, I do. I doubt if *work* is a four-letter word to you.'

'Speaking as a professor of Linguistics,' he snarled, 'I can assure you that work is indeed a four-letter word.' As he reached for the ashtray, his dressing gown fell open, revealing withered nipples and grey matted chest hair. I was almost physically sick. I could hardly swallow my Bran Flakes.

Took the portable TV back to the shop. On my return, I wrote a poem to Pandora and slipped it under her door. It was my last-ditch attempt to seduce her away from Cavendish.

Pandora! Let Me! by A. Mole
Let me stroke your inner thighs
Let me hear your breathy sighs
Let me feel your silky skin
Let me make your senses spin
Let me touch your soft white breast
Let us stop and have a rest.
Let me join our beating hearts
Let me forge our private parts
Let me delve and make you mine
Let me give you food and wine
Let me lick you with my tongue
Let me do whatever's wrong
Let me watch you take your pleasure
Let me dress you in black leather
Let me fit you like a glove
Let me consummate our love.

At 1 a.m. Pandora pushed a note under my door.

> Adrian,
> If you continue to send such filth to me, I will, in future,
> pass it on to the police.
>
> Pandora

Saturday March 2nd

As I packed my belongings, I reflected that I have not acquired much in my life. A basic wardrobe of clothes. A few hundred books. A Sony Walkman. A dozen or so cassettes. My own mug, cup, bowl and plate. A poster by Munch, a cactus, a magnifying mirror on a stand, a bowl for bananas, and a lamp. It is not much to show for a year and a half of toil at the D.O.E. True, I have got £2,579 saved in the Market Harborough Building Society, and £197.39 in Nat West, but even so.

I found the blue plastic comb I have been searching for since last year. It was on top of the wardrobe. Why? How did it get there? I have never climbed on the wardrobe to comb my hair. I suspect Julian. He is a big fan of Jeremy Beadle's.

11 p.m. Too tired to write much, just to put it on the record that I am lying in Mrs Hedge's bed. It is very comfortable. My new address is now:

> 8 Sitwell Villas
> Summertown
> Oxford.

Sunday March 3rd

I didn't know where I was when I woke up, then I remembered. I smelt bacon cooking, but I didn't go downstairs. I felt like an intruder. I got up, tiptoed to the bathroom, got dressed, made my bed, then sat on the bed listening to sounds from below. Eventually, driven by hunger, I went downstairs. Mrs Hedge was not there. The breakfast plates were still on the kitchen table. The kitchen pedal bin was overflowing. There were egg-shells on the floor. The cupboard under the sink was full of filthy yellow dusters. The fridge was full of little saucers containing mouldy leftovers. The grill pan was unwashed. The *Observer* was speckled with tinned tomato juice.

It is as I feared: Mrs Hedge is a slut. The phone rang non-stop. Took messages: 'Ted phoned.' 'Ian rang.' 'Martin called.' 'Call Kingsley back.' 'Julian rang: Are you going to the launch on Tuesday?'

I was mopping the kitchen floor when Mrs Hedge returned. She was carrying a large shrub and four tins of Carlsberg.

'Christ,' she said. 'It looks like I've struck lucky. Do you like housework, Mr Mole?'

'I find it difficult to tolerate disorder,' I said.

She went out into the garden to plant the shrub, then sat on the patio on an iron chair, swigging Carlsberg out of the tin. She didn't seem to notice the cold. When it started to rain, she came into the house, got a golfing umbrella from the jar in the hall, and went back out again. I went up to my room to work on my novel, *Lo! The Flat Hills of My Homeland*.

When I next went downstairs, there was no sign of Mrs Hedge. I was pleased to see three tins of Carlsberg still left in the fridge. She may be a slut and an eccentric, but, thank God, she is not yet an alcoholic.

Monday   March 4th

Mrs Hedge was still in bed when I got back from work. The kitchen was a disgrace. The Carlsberg was gone from the fridge. She must have drunk them in bed! It is the only conclusion.

Wednesday   March 6th

Went to Pandora's to pick up my post. Nothing exciting. Letters from the Market Harborough Building Society, *Reader's Digest* and Plumbs, a firm promoting stretch covers. How did Plumbs get hold of my name and address? I have never shown the slightest interest in soft furnishings. Pandora has turned my box room into a study. I opened a file on her desk marked, 'Lecture Notes'. Didn't understand a word. They were written in what was probably Serbo-Croat.

Thursday   March 7th

I walked into the bathroom tonight without knocking. Mrs Hedge was in the bath, shaving her legs. I will buy a bolt for the door tomorrow. I'd guess she is at least 38C.

Friday   March 8th

Mrs Hedge said, 'Feel free to invite your friends round, Mr Mole.' I told her that I hadn't got any friends. I walk alone.

When I told Leonora the same thing, she said, 'Before our next session, please try to speak to a stranger; smile and initiate a conversation; and make a new female friend.'

Saturday   March 9th

There was a stranger in the kitchen when I came down. He was eating Marmite on toast. He said, 'Hi. I'm Gerry.'

I smiled and said, 'Good morning. I'm Adrian Mole.'

That was the extent of our social intercourse. I found it difficult to initiate a conversation with a man wearing a woman's negligé and nothing else.

I made myself a cup of tea and left.

I wish I was back in my box room.

Monday   March 11th

Mr Major on the news. He said, 'I want us to be where we belong, at the very heart of Europe, working with our partners in building the future.'

A peculiar thing: Mr Major cannot say the word 'want' to rhyme with 'font', which is the correct English pronunciation. For some reason, he says '*went*'. I suspect that this disability stems from childhood. When little John lisped, 'I want some sweeties,' etc.,etc. Did his father leap down from his trapeze and shout, 'I'll give you *want*!'? Or shout, 'Say *want* again and I'll beat you black and blue,' thus leaving little John sobbing into the sawdust of the Big Top and unable to pronounce that little English word?

My heart goes out to him. He is obviously in urgent need of therapy. It seems to me that we have both suffered for having embarrassing fathers. I will bring the subject up when I next see Leonora.

Tuesday   March 12th

Brown slipped down a grassy bank and bruised his coccyx at the weekend. He was collecting owl droppings. He has been incapacitated and is lying on a plank on his bedroom floor. Ha! Ha! Ha! Ho! Ho! Ho! Three cheers!

Wednesday   March 13th

Brown's deputy, Gordon Goffe, is throwing his weight (twenty stone) about. He is conducting an enquiry into 'postage stamp pilfering'. This is just my luck. I was about to send the opening chapters of my novel *Lo! The Flat Hills of My Homeland* off to Faber and Faber today. I shall have to fork out for the stamps myself. Once they have read these chapters, they will be panting for the rest.

Thursday   March 14th

The Birmingham Six have been released from prison.

Gordon Goffe is lumbering around the offices, carrying out spot checks on our drawers. Megan was found to have an illicit box of D.O.E. ballpoints. She has received an oral warning. No session with Leonora this week. She is attending a conference in Sacramento.

Friday   March 15th

Barry Kent was on *Kaleidoscope* reading from *Dork's Diary*. The little I heard was nihilistic rubbish. Goffe barged into my cubicle and said that I was not allowed to listen to Radio Four during office hours. I pointed out that Mr Brown had never objected.

Goffe said, 'I am not Mr Brown,' a statement so stupid that I was lost for an answer. I've got an answer now, at three minutes past midnight, but it is obviously too late.

Saturday   March 16th

Called round to Pandora's flat for my letters. Nothing of interest: circular for thermal underwear; *Reader's Digest* competition entry form – prize: a gold bar; Plumbs catalogue, offering discount on mock velvet curtains. I am twenty-four next month and I must confess, dear journal, that I had expected by now to be in correspondence with interesting and fascinating people. Instead, the world seems to think of me as a person who gets up in the morning, puts on his thermal underwear, draws his mock velvet curtains and settles down to read his new copy of *Reader's Digest*.

The cat looked thin, but was pleased to see me. I gave it a whole tin of cat food. Pandora was out, so I had a good look around the flat. Her underwear drawer is full of disgusting sex aids. Bluebeard is obviously not up to it.

Sunday   March 17th

Had an interesting talk about the Russian elections with the girl in the local newsagent's this morning. Then, as she handed me my *Sunday Times*, she remarked (joking, I presume), 'It's very heavy. Would you like me to help you carry it home?'

'No,' I jocularly replied. 'I think I can just about manage.' Though, as I took it, I pretended to buckle under its weight. How we laughed.

She is quite pleasant-looking in a sort of unassuming sort of way.

6.00 p.m. On rereading the above, I think I have been unfair to the girl in the newsagent's. A gingham nylon overall is not the most flattering of garments. And I didn't see her legs, as they were behind the counter at all times.

I have just read the *Sunday Times* Books section and was appalled, astonished and disgusted to see that *Dork's Diary* is at number ten in the hardback bestseller list today!

Monday   March 18th

Called in at the newsagent's for a packet of Polos on the way to work. The girl joked that I was paying for fresh air, i.e. the hole! This hadn't occurred to me before, so I handed the Polos back to her and said, 'Okay, I'll have Trebor Mints instead.' Again, we laughed uproariously. She has certainly got a good sense of humour. Legs still behind the counter. Brown still malingering at home. Goffe still rampaging in the office. Leonora will be pleased to hear about the girl in the newsagent's.

Tuesday   March 19th

A letter from Pandora, my first at Sitwell Villas:

Sunday, March 17th

Adrian,
I have asked you many times to return the front door key to this flat. You have not yet done so. I'm afraid I must give you an ultimatum. Either the key is in my possession by 7 p.m. on Tuesday night, or I call out a locksmith, have the lock changed and send the bill to you. The choice is yours. I will no longer tolerate you:
   a) interfering in the cat's feeding pattern;

b) snooping in my underwear drawer; or
c) helping yourself to food from the refrigerator
   when I am not there.

As I have said, I will continue to redirect your post
(such as it is) and relay any messages that I consider to be
urgent.

At 6.59 p.m., I pushed an envelope containing the key, a ten-
pence piece and a terse note under the door of Pandora's flat.
The note said:

Pandora,
a) In my opinion, the cat is too thin and appears to
   be lacking in energy;
b) I vividly remember you saying that 'Suspenders, etc.
   are symbols of women's enslavement to men's lust.'
   Ditto vibrators;
c) The pot of crab paste in the refrigerator was *mine*.
   I purchased it on February 20th this year. I have the
   receipt to prove it. I admit that I did help myself to a
   slice of bread. I enclose, as you cannot fail to see, a ten-
   pence coin, as remuneration for the slice of granary.

Wednesday   March 20th

How do I get the legs out from behind the counter?

Thursday   March 21st

Her name is Bianca. A strange name for somebody working in
a newsagent's. They are usually called Joyce. I saw her carrying
boxes of crisps from a delivery lorry into the shop. Legs okay,
but ankles a bit bony, so, on a scale of one to ten, only five.

9.00 p.m. Leonora was in a strange mood tonight. She was
annoyed because I was fifteen minutes late. I pointed out to
her that she would be paid for the full hour.

She said, 'That's not the point, Adrian. Our sessions together
are carefully structured. I insist that you are punctual in future.'

I replied, 'My chronic unpunctuality is one of my many
problems. Shouldn't you be addressing it?'

She crossed her shapely legs under her black silk skirt and I saw a flash of white. From that point on I was helpless and could only nod or shake my head in answer to her questions. Speech was beyond me. I felt that if I opened my mouth I would utter crude inarticulate protestations of lust, which would frighten her and signal the end of our time together.

Ten minutes before the end of our session she said, 'You are displaying typically regressive behaviour at the moment, shall we take advantage of it?'

I nodded and she encouraged me to talk about my earliest memories. I remembered being bitten by a dog and my grandma applying iodine to the wound. I also remember my (now dead) grandad kicking the dog round the kitchen.

Then it was time to fork out £30 and leave.

Saturday March 23rd

Mrs Hedge asked me if she should marry Gerry, sell up and move to Cardiff. I advised against it. I have only just settled in, found out how to work the grill pan, etc. I can't face looking for alternative accommodation. Anyway, why ask me? I've only spoken to the ugly brute a few times.

Sunday March 24th

The lavatory seat was up, so I guessed that Gerry was *in situ*. I went to buy my newspaper from Bianca and, on my return, sure enough, Gerry and Mrs Hedge were in the kitchen eating eggs and bacon. Mrs Hedge didn't look pleased to see me. I threw a few Rice Krispies into a bowl and took them up to my room. But, by the time I'd got upstairs, they had stopped snapping and crackling and popping, which annoyed me considerably. I loathe soggy cereals.

Monday March 25th

Gerry is now a fixture. I am like a cuckoo in the nest. A gooseberry in the strawberry patch. A piranha in the goldfish bowl. Conversation stops when I enter the kitchen or sitting room and they are there. I wanted to watch the Oscar ceremony

on television tonight, but Gerry snatched the remote control and
kept it on his lap, thus denying me the pleasure of *seeing* that
gifted and modest actor Jeremy Irons win an Oscar for Britain. I
had to hear this wonderful news on Radio Four and visualise Mr
Irons's delight myself. Whoever said that the 'pictures are better on
the radio' was completely wrong.

Tuesday   March 26th

I have asked Bianca to give me prior warning, should a suitable-
sounding postcard arrive at the shop offering accommodation.
She agreed. I think she finds me personable. Haste has changed
the meaning of the above sentence: postcards cannot walk into
a newsagent's and talk suitably. Leonora cancelled tonight's
appointment. 'An emergency,' she said.

Am I not an emergency? My sanity hangs by a gossamer
thread. Leonora is the only barrier between me and the public
ward in a lunatic asylum. How will she live with herself if I am
admitted foaming at the mouth and struggling inside a strait-
jacket?

Wednesday   March 27th

Mr David Icke, who is a famous Leicester person, has revealed
that he is a 'channel for the Christ spirit'. He went on television
and told the goggling press that his wife and daughter were 'in-
carnations of the archangel Michael'. He blamed the planet Sirus
for bringing earthquakes and pestilence to the world. Gerry and
Mrs Hedge mocked him and said he is barmy, but I'm not so
sure. We Leicester people are known for our level heads. Perhaps
Mr Icke knows something that we ordinary mortals cannot even
guess at.

Thursday   March 28th

Bianca studied Astronomy in the sixth form. She said this morning, 'There is no such planet as Sirus.' But, as I pointed out to
her, 'David Icke did say that Sirus was *undiscovered*, so naturally no reference *would* be found to it in the books, would it?'

A queue formed, so we were forced to break off our

discussion. I called in on my way home from work, but Bianca was busy – some old git was complaining about his newspaper bill.

Friday   March 29th

The more I think about David Icke's predictions, i.e. that the world will end unless it 'purges itself of evil', the more it makes sense. He is a successful man, who was employed by the BBC, no less! He was also a professional goalkeeper for Hereford City. We should not be too quick to scoff. Columbus was once mocked for remarking that the world was round. Something that was verified by the first U.S. astronauts.

My mother rang tonight to ask me what I want for my birthday next week. I told her to get me the usual, a book token. She went on to say that Leicester was agog about David Icke, and that 'there has been a run on turquoise track suits' (worn by Mr Icke's followers). She said she felt sorry for his mother. Apparently, Mr Icke claimed he was born on the planet Sirus, whereas his mother said in the *Leicester Mercury* that she distinctly remembers giving birth to him in the Leicester General Maternity Hospital.

I ran out of bananas tonight. I had to walk to the outer suburbs before finding an off-licence that stocked them.

Saturday   March 30th

Posted two birthday cards to myself. I put second-class stamps on, so they should get here by Tuesday morning.

Monday   April 1st

A man with a Glaswegian accent rang me in my cubicle this morning and said, 'I have just finished reading the opening chapters of your novel *Lo! The Flat Hills of My Homeland* and I want to publish it next year. Would an advance of £50,000 be acceptable?'

I stammered out, 'Yes,' and asked to whom I was speaking.

'*A. Fool!*' laughed the imposter, and slammed the phone down.

How cruel can you get? For fifteen seconds, I had achieved my ambition. I was a professional writer living in my own house. I'd learned to drive. I had a car in the garage. I had a Rolex watch and a Mont Blanc pen. There was an air ticket to the U.S.A. in the pocket of my cashmere coat. Fan letters bristled inside my leather briefcase. Invitations to literary events were stacked on the mantelpiece. Then my dream was shattered by the hoaxer and I went back to being simple Adrian Mole, who was halfway through writing a report on newt movements, in a cubicle in a D.O.E. building in Oxford. I suspect Goffe.

Tuesday   April 2nd

Birthday cards from Mother, Rosie, Father, Grandma, Mrs Hedge and Megan. Six cards in all. Not bad. I needn't have posted two to myself.

> *Presents*
> 1) Ten pound book token from mother.
> 2) W. H. Smith voucher from father (fiver).
> 3) 2 pairs of socks from Mrs Hedge (white).
> 4) Cactus plant from Megan (obscene).

No surprise party. No candles to blow out. No singing. No Leonora until Thursday.

Wednesday April 3rd

I am twenty-four and one day old. *Question:* What have I done with my life? *Answer:* Nothing.

Graham Greene died today. I wrote to him four years ago, pointing out a grammatical error in his book, *The Human Factor*. He didn't reply.

Thursday April 4th

I trimmed my beard this morning. Mrs Hedge screamed when I came out of the bathroom. When she recovered, she said, 'Christ, you look like the Yorkshire Ripper.'

I had a terrible session with Leonora. I went into her room with the self-esteem of an anorexic aphid and came out feeling worse.

My low self-esteem on entering Leonora's room was due to an acrimonious phone conversation I'd had with my mother earlier. She had rung the office to ask me if I would like to go to a party given by Barry Kent to celebrate the success of *Dork's Diary*. The venue is the North East Leicester Working Men's Club, and half of Leicester has been invited.

I said to my mother, 'I would sooner wash a corpse.'

My mother accused me of petty jealousy, and then had a tantrum and recited my faults: arrogance, overweening pride, snobbery, pretension, phoney intellectualism, wimpishness, etc., etc.

I recited this to Leonora who said, 'I suggest that you take on board what your mother is saying. I also suggest that you *go to the party*.' She said that she had bought five copies of *Dork's Diary*: for her husband, Fergus; for her best friend, Susan Strachan; for her therapist, Simon; for her supervisor, Alison; and for herself. I was totally gobsmacked. When Leonora said that it was time to go, I refused to leave my chair.

I said, 'I can't bear the thought of you enjoying Barry Kent's work.'

Leonora said, 'Tough, give me thirty pounds and leave.'

I said, 'No, I am totally sexually obsessed by you. I think about you constantly. I have revealed my innermost feelings to you.'

Leonora said, 'Yours is a standard reaction. You'll get over it.'

I said, 'Leonora, I feel betrayed. I refuse to be treated like an example from a text book.'

Leonora stood up and tossed her magnificent head and said, 'Ours is a professional relationship, Mr Mole. It could never be anything else. Come and see me next Thursday.'

'Okay,' I said. 'Take your thirty pieces of silver.'

I flung a Market Harborough Building Society cheque made out for thirty pounds onto the desk and left, slamming the door.

If my father had allowed me to abandon that dummy in my own time, I'm convinced I would now be enjoying perfect mental health.

Saturday April 6th

Am I the only person in Britain who has an open mind re the David Icke sensation? Bianca described him as a 'barmpot' this morning – but as I pointed out to her, Jesus himself was reviled in his day. The press were against him and the money-lenders slagged him off to all and sundry. Also, Jesus was a bit of an eccentric as regards clothes. He would not have won a 'Best Dressed Palestinian of the Year Award'. But, had track suits been around in Christ's day, he would almost certainly have opted for the comfort and washability of such garments.

Sunday April 7th

Dork's Diary is now at number eight. Glanced through my *Illustrated Bible Stories* tonight and was startled to find on page 33 (Raising Lazarus) that Jesus is wearing turquoise robes!!!

Monday April 8th

Brown is back, but he is wearing a noisy surgical corset, which is quite useful (the noise, not the corset), because Megan is seeing Bill Blane (Badger Dept) on the side. I like Bill. He and I discussed David Icke at the Autovent today. Bill agrees with me that Sirus could have been overlooked by the astronomers. It could well have been hidden behind another, bigger planet.

The emir of Kuwait has promised to hold parliamentary elections next year. He has announced that women will be allowed to vote. Good for you, Sir!

Tuesday   April 9th

John Major has been cross-examined by the press about his
'O' levels. I hope this won't remind Brown about my own, non-
existent, Biology 'A' level. Why, oh why, couldn't I have been born
an American? College students there are given multiple choice
type exams. All the dumbos have to do is put a tick against what
they think is the right answer.

> *Example:*   Question: Who discovered America?
> Was it: a) Columbus?
>   b) Mickey Mouse?
>   c) Rambo?

Wednesday   April 10th

Bill Blane has asked me to go for a drink after work tomorrow.
This could be the start of a new friendship.

Thursday   April 11th

Bill wanted to talk about Megan. In fact, he talked about her
all night. I couldn't get a word in edgeways, apart from saying,
'Same again?' when it was my turn to buy a round. I drank far
too much (three pints) and in my muddled state started walking
back to Pandora's flat before realising my mistake and turning
my steps towards the Hedge household.

Friday   April 12th

Worked on *Lo! The Flat Hills of My Homeland* tonight. Started
Chapter Eleven:

> As he skirted the top of the hill, he looked east and
> saw the city of Leicester glowing in the dying embers
> of the setting sun. The tower blocks reflected the scarlet
> rays and bounced them against the factory chimneys and
> the Royal Infirmary multi-storey car park. He sighed with
> the glorious anticipation of knowing that he would soon be
> tramping the reconstituted concrete streets of his home
> town. He could have entered the city by a more discreet
> route – turned off the motorway at Junction 23 – but he

preferred this, the route of the sheep drovers, and anyway, he hadn't got a car.

He had been away too long, he thought. He had grown tired of the world and its attractions. Leicester was where his heart was. He strode down the hill, his eyes were wet. The wind, perhaps? Or the pain of absence? He would never know. The sun slipped away behind the grand edifice of the Alliance and Leicester Building Society headquarters and he felt the stealthy black fingers of night collect around him. Soon it was dark. Still he descended. Down. Down.

Not many people know that Leicester lies in a basin, he ruminated. No wonder it is the bronchitis centre of the world, he thought. Before long, he had descended the hill and he was on flat ground.

I think this is probably the best writing I have ever done. It is magnificent. I hope I can maintain this standard throughout the novel.

Saturday   April 13th

Notes on *Lo!:*

a) Should I give my hero a name? Or should I continue to call him '*he*', '*him*', etc.?

b) Should the narrative be stronger? At the moment, not much happens. *He* leaves Leicester, then comes back to Leicester. Should the reader know what *he* does in between?

c) Should *he* have sex, or go shopping? Most modern novels are full of references to one or the other – the reading public obviously relishes such activities.

Descriptions (to be slotted in somewhere):

The tree bent in the wind, like a pensioner at Land's End.

The fried egg spluttered in the frying pan like an old man having a tubercular coughing fit in a 1930s National Health Service hospital.

Her breasts were as full as hot air balloons.

Her face was infused with anger, her eyes flashed
like a manic lighthouse whose wick needed cleaning.

The tea was welcome. *He* sipped it gratefully, like
an African elephant which has previously found its
waterhole to be dry, but then remembered, and walked
to, another.

From now on, I shall write down these thoughts and ideas as
they come to me. They are far too good to waste. Publication
looks to be within my grasp.

Sunday   April 14th

Woke at 8.30, had breakfast: cornflakes, toast, brown sauce, two
cups of tea. Collected *Sunday Times* and *Observer*. Bianca not
there. *Dork's Diary* has gone to number seven. Changed into
blazer. Walked round Outer Ring Road, came back. Brushed and
hung up blazer. Lay on bed. Slept. Woke up, put on blazer, went
out, had pizza in Pizza Hut. Came back, lay on bed, slept. Woke,
had bath, changed into pyjamas and dressing gown. Cut toenails,
trimmed beard, inspected skin. Tidied tapes into alphabetical
order, Abba to Warsaw Concerto. Went downstairs. Mrs Hedge in
kitchen, in tears at kitchen table. 'I've got nobody to confide
in,' she cried. Made crab paste sandwiches. Went to bed. Wrote
up journal.
  I can't go on like this; I'd have more of a social life in prison.

Monday   April 15th

Went to see D.O.E. doctor, Dr Abrahams. I told him I was
depressed. He told me he was depressed. I told him that my
life was meaningless, that my ambitions remained unrealised. He
told me that his dream was to become the Queen's gynaecologist
by the age of 44. I asked him how old he was. He told me that he
was 45. Poor old git. He gave me a prescription for my depres-
sion. I asked the chemist if there were any side effects.
  She said, 'Well, there's lack of concentration. Your physical
movement may be reduced. You'll notice an increase in heart
rate. There'll possibly be sweating and tremors, constipation and
perhaps difficulty in urinating. Bit depressing, really, isn't it?'
  I agreed with her and tore the prescription into pieces.

Wednesday   April 17th

Rocky gave me a lift to work this morning in his limo. We discussed Pandora, how arrogant she is, etc. Rocky said, 'But, y'know, Aid, I'll always love the girl, she's, y'know, kinda like *unique*.'

I congratulated Rocky on his use of the word 'unique'.

Rocky told me that Carly Pick, his girl friend, is teaching him new words.

I said, 'So, she's extending your vocabulary, is she?' But he looked at me blankly, from which I inferred that she hadn't been at it for long.

When the car drew up outside the D.O.E., I was pleased to see that Brown was looking out of his office window. He ducked out of sight, but he couldn't have failed to see me exiting from the limousine. It won't hurt Brown to know that I mingle with the rich and powerful.

Robert Maxwell has saved the *Mirror*. He is a saint!

Thursday   April 18th

The Newport Pagnell newts seem to have settled down, thank God. The road plans are finalised and construction is due to start next month.

Mrs Brown came to the office today. She had lost her handbag in the Ashmolean Museum. Brown was entirely unsympathetic. Before he closed his office door, I heard him say, 'That's the second time this year, you stupid cow.' He would not have spoken to Megan like that. Mrs Brown is very pretty. It's just that her clothes are horrible. It's as though there is a lunatic living in her wardrobe who orders her what to wear every morning. She can get away with looking ridiculous in Oxford. People probably assume that she is just another barmy professor, but she would be a laughing stock in Leicester.

Saturday   April 20th

Mrs Hedge crying again this morning. I must away from this Vale of Tears. I need cheerful people around me.

Bianca handed me a card this morning. It said, in mad handwriting:

ROOM TO LET

Academic household willing to let room free to tolerant person of either gender, in return for light household duties/babysitting/cat-sitting. Would suit working person with most evenings free. Please ring Dr Palmer.

I rang immediately from the phone box outside the newsagent's. A bloke answered.

DR PALMER: Christian Palmer speaking.

ME: Dr Palmer, my name is Adrian Mole. I've just seen your postcard in the newsagent's.

DR P: When can you start?

ME: Start what?

DR P: Looking after the bloody kids.

ME: But you don't know me.

DR P: You sound okay and you've already proved you can use a telephone. So you can't be a total simpleton. Have you got all your faculties: four limbs, eyesight?

ME: Yes.

DR P: Ever been done for molesting kiddiewinkies?

ME: No.

DR P: Got any particularly nasty personal habits?

ME: No.

DR P: Good. So when can you start? I'm on my own here. My wife's in the States.

The telephone receiver was dropped. Suddenly I heard Palmer shout, 'Tamsin, put the top back on that bottle of bleach! Now!'

He came back on the phone and gave me his address in Banbury Road.

I went into the newsagent's and asked Bianca what newspapers and magazines Palmer read. This is a sure sign of character. It was a baffling list:

Newspapers: *The Observer, The Daily Telegraph, The Sun, The Washington Post, The Oxford Mail, The Independent, The Sunday Times, Today.*

Magazines: *Time Out, Private Eye, Just Seventeen, Vogue, Brides, Forum, Computer Weekly, Woman's Own, Paris Match, Gardening Today, Hello!, The Spectator, The Literary Review, Socialist Outpost,*

The Beano, Angler's Weekly, Canoeist, Viz, Interiors, Goal!

I stopped her and said, 'Palmer's newspaper bill must be enormous. How does he pay it?'

'Infrequently,' she replied.

Sunday April 21st

Dr Palmer is tall and thin and wears his hair like Elvis Presley did during his silver-cloaks-in-Los-Angeles phase. His first words to me were, 'On your way to a fancy dress party?' He laughed and fingered the lapels of my blazer.

I mumbled something neutral and he asked, 'Is that beard *real*?'

I assured him that I had grown it myself and he said, 'How old are you?'

I answered, 'Twenty-four,' and he laughed a strange laugh, like a dog's bark, and said, '*Twenty-four:* so why the hell do you want to walk round looking like bloody Jack Hawkins?'

'Who's Jack Hawkins?' I asked.

'He's a film star,' he replied. 'Everybody's heard of Jack Hawkins.' He looked annoyed for some reason. Then he said, 'Well, unless you're twenty-four, that is.'

We were still standing on the doorstep of his decrepit house. A line of dirty, unrinsed milk bottles stood on the step. A little kid of unknown sex ran up the hall and tugged at Palmer's trousers. 'I've done a great big one! Come and look, Daddy!' it said.

We all three went into a gigantic room which seemed to be a kitchen, living-room and study combined. In the middle of the floor stood a potty in the shape of an elephant. Dr Palmer looked in the potty and exclaimed, 'Tamsin, that is a truly wonderful piece of shit.'

I averted my eyes as he carried the potty out of the room. Then I heard him shouting, 'Alpha! Griffith! Come and see what Tamsin's done!' There was a thundering on the stairs. I looked into the hall and saw two other androgynous children looking into the potty, saying, 'Wow!' and 'Mega shit!'

I adjusted my blazer in the mirror over the large fireplace and thought that the Dr Palmer household was unsuited to one of my temperament. I do not like to hear little children swear and I prefer them to be dressed in proper clothes and to have hairstyles which give a clue to their sexual orientation. However, when Dr Palmer came back from emptying the potty, I was pleased to see that he was drying his hands, which indicated to me that he knew the fundamentals of hygiene. I agreed to inspect the free room. We climbed the stairs, followed by Tamsin, Griffith and Alpha, who spoke to each other in a language I was not familiar with.

'Is it Welsh they're speaking?' I asked.

'No,' Palmer laughed. 'It's Oombagoomba. It's their own language. They're wearing their Oombagoomba clothes.'

I looked at the rags and bits of cloth and shawls, etc. with which the kids were festooned and was relieved to find out that it was not their usual mode of dress. I too used to have my own made-up language (Ikbak), until my father beat it out of me during a long car journey to Skegness.

The 'free room' turned out to be the whole of the attic floor. It had a kitchen at one end, and a private bathroom at the other. There was a proper desk. I could imagine reading the proofs of *Lo!* at that desk.

'You can do what you like up here,' said Palmer, 'apart from serial killing.'

'Are you a teacher?' I ventured.

'No,' he said. 'I'm leading a research project on popular culture. We are trying to establish why people go out to pubs, discos, bingo sessions, to the cinema, that sort of thing.'

'It's to enjoy themselves, isn't it?' I said.

Palmer laughed again. 'Yeah, but I've got to stretch that very simplistic answer into a three-year study and a seven-hundred page book.'

As we went down the stairs, I mentioned to Dr Palmer that as well as being an excellent tenant, I am also a novelist and a poet.

He groaned and said, 'So long as you *never* ask me to look at your manuscripts, we'll stay the best of friends.'

He made me a cup of coffee after grinding up some beans and he told me a bit about his wife, Cassandra, who is in Los Angeles directing a film about mutilation. She sounds horrific, although he claims to miss her. I am too tired and confused to write more. Dr Palmer has told me he must know by Wednesday if I want the room. He's got to go out on Friday to a darts competition.

Monday   April 22nd

Should I go, or should I stay?

Can I stand babysitting for three children, four nights a week?

I could save £75 a week. In a year, that is . . . ? As usual, when faced with mental, or even physical, arithmetic, my brain has just left my body and walked out of the room.

Thank God for calculators. Nine hundred pounds! It's not as if I would be sacrificing my social life. I haven't got one and, with a bit of luck, Mrs Palmer will stay in America, or fall over Niagara Falls, or something.

Thursday   April 25th

Rang Palmer from the office and told him that I would be moving in tonight. Rang Pandora; asked if Cavendish would help me to move.

'Moving?' she said. 'Again?' Then, 'You make more moves than a tiddlywink.'

Rang Mrs Hedge, asked her to take my Y-fronts out of the washer and hang them on my bedroom radiator to dry. Mentioned that I would be moving on.

She said, 'Everybody does, eventually.'

Rang my mother and gave her my new address in case of a family tragedy. She yakked on for half an hour about President Gorbachev's threat to resign and predicted that the U.S.S.R. was in danger of collapse. I cut in eventually and said, 'I no longer take an interest in world events. There is nothing I can do to influence them, so why bother?'

Rang Grandma, in Leicester. Had a long chat about Princess Diana. Grandma doesn't think she's been looking happy lately. I voiced my own concern. Diana is too thin.

Rang Market Harborough Building Society to notify change of address.

Rang Waterstone's. Pretended to be irate reader; threatened to sue them for selling pornography, i.e. *Dork's Diary*.

Rang Megan. Pretended to be Brown. Said, 'God, I love you, Megan,' in his horrible squeaky voice.

Eventually, Brown burst in and demanded that I get off the phone. I sincerely hope he hasn't been listening outside the door.

I had a compulsion to visit Leonora again. She agreed to see me immediately. She was wearing a white dress. She looked like a sacrificial virgin. I wanted to deflower her, but I found myself talking about Bianca. Leonora leant forward in her chair, displaying her dark cleavage. I found myself saying that I was quite interested in Bianca, although I found her lack of cleavage disappointing.

Leonora said, 'But could you love Bianca?'

I said, 'The idea is ridiculous. The thought of *her* doesn't keep me awake at night, but the thought of *you* does.'

Leonora sighed and said, 'I suggest you cultivate this friendship with Bianca. I am a married woman, Adrian. Your obsession with me is typical of a therapist/client relationship. It is called transference. You must face the truth about your feelings.'

I said, 'The truth about my feelings is that I don't love you. I just want to go to bed with you.'

Leonora said, 'Thirty pounds please.'

I felt like a client paying a whore.

Friday   April 26th

MOVING DAY

Cavendish and Palmer are old friends. When they saw each other, they did that arms-clasped-on-each-other's-shoulders, then grin-and-shake, which so many men in Oxford seem to go in for these days. As I removed my possessions from the back of the Volvo and tried to stop Tamsin, Griffith and Alpha from interfering, I heard Cavendish and Palmer laughing like madmen in the living-room. I'm not sure, but I think I heard the word 'blazer' mentioned. The children spoke Oombagoomba all night until their father returned at 11.30 p.m. They flatly refused to go to bed, or to converse with me in English. Instead, they lay under the massive pine table on a pile of cushions and jabbered away in that made-up lingo. It was like being abroad; if you closed your eyes.

Saturday   April 27th

Bought *The White Hotel* by D. M. Thomas this morning. If it is even half as good as *The Great Babylon Hotel* by Arnold Bennett I will be more than satisfied. When Christian saw me take it out of the carrier bag, he raised his eyebrows and said, 'Don't leave it lying around. Alpha's got a reading age of thirteen.'

I said, 'You should encourage your child to read.'

Christian snapped, '*The White Hotel* is a bit heavy for a kid who still believes that fairies live at the bottom of the garden.'

I must say this surprised me. I went down to the bottom of the garden yesterday. It is covered in rusting toys and stinking garden rubbish. It is hardly Fairyland.

At 11.30 p.m., I opened *The White Hotel*, read for ten minutes, then got out of bed and bolted the door. It must never fall into Alpha's hands.

Monday   April 29th

Babysat. Christian is at the semi-final of a darts competition with his dictaphone and clipboard. Do the big-bellied darts players realise that they are taking part in a research project? I doubt it. They all seem to have tunnel vision, which I suppose is an advantage if you play darts for a living.

Christian told me today that Bianca was enquiring about me, asking if I'd settled in. He told her that the kids like me. I wish he'd told me. Christian asked me why I don't ask Bianca for a date. I answered nonchalantly that I was too busy. But, dear journal, the truth is that I'm afraid *she might refuse*. My ego is but a frail and fragile thing and furthermore am I sure I want to commit myself to a person who works in a newsagent's shop?

Notes on Bianca:

Negative

1. She is pleasant-looking but certainly not a head-turner, unlike Leonora, who is capable of stopping the traffic.
2. When I mentioned that my walk to work was 'pleasantly Chekhovian', largely due to the blossoming cherry trees, she looked at me blankly and asked me what 'Chekhovian' meant.
3. Her hips do not look capable of bearing a child.
4. She wears Doc Marten boots.
5. She is a Guns 'n' Roses fan.

Positive

1. She is kind, especially to the children who linger over the sweets section in the newsagent's.
2. I seem to be able to make her laugh.
3. Her skin looks like white silk. I have a strange desire to stroke her face whenever I am close to her.

Tuesday   April 30th

I'm glad April is over. It is a bitter-sweet month. The blossom is out, but the wind still swells around and flaps the bottoms of your trousers unless you tuck them into your socks.

Beard bushy now. Food gets caught in it. Brown pointed out a piece of egg white at 9.30 a.m. I ate my boiled egg at 7.39 this morning. Since that time, I have spoken to, or been seen by, at least thirty people. Why did no one else point out that I had egg white in my beard? It is not as if it was a *small* piece. As egg white goes, it was quite a large piece, and as such, impossible to overlook. I will have to buy a small hand mirror and check my beard regularly after meals. I cannot risk such social embarrassment happening again.

Wednesday   May 1st

Babysat. Griffith asked me to help him with his model of a Scud missile, which he is making out of a toilet roll tube and cut-up bits of washing-up liquid bottle. I pointed out to him that I am a pacifist.

Griffith (six) said, 'If your sister was being threatened by a gang of vicious thugs, would you stand by and do nothing?'

I said, 'Yes.' Griffith doesn't know my sister Rosie. She is quite capable of seeing off a gang of vicious thugs.

Christian was back from his karaoke evening by 11 p.m. Apparently, he'd been forced to sing 'Love is a Many Splendoured Thing' in order to keep his cover. So his research project *is* an undercover operation. That explains why Christian changes out of his ragged denims and into his Sta-Pressed polyesters before joining his unsuspecting fellow low-culture vultures.

Thursday   May 2nd

Read through the whole of *Lo! The Flat Hills of My Homeland* manuscript so far. It is crap from start to finish.

Friday   May 3rd

Perhaps I was too harsh last night. *Lo!* has passages of sheer brilliance. About five.

Saturday   May 4th

Left *Lo!* on kitchen table overnight. No comment from Christian this morning, though Alpha said, 'You've spelt "success" wrong on page four. It's got two c's and two s's.' Christian didn't even look up from his *Sun*.

If there's one thing I can't bear, it's a precocious child. It's completely unnatural. I was tempted to tell Alpha that any fairy living in the Hell Hole at the bottom of her garden should have a tetanus jab, but I didn't.

I received the new Plumbs catalogue this morning, offering me four tapestry-look cushions with frilled edges at the bargain price of £27.99. How did they track me down? The envelope came direct from Plumbs to the Banbury Road. Are they watching me?

Sunday   May 5th

Put blazer on and went for my customary Sunday walk around the Outer Ring Road at 2 p.m. Some old git in a Morris Minor stopped and asked me for directions to the Oxford Bowling Club. As if *I*'d know! Returned to find house full of Christian's friends having what he described as a 'fondue party'. They were dipping raw vegetables into a stinking pot of what looked like yellow emulsion paint. I declined to join them.

Monday   May 6th

Bianca was passing as I left for work this morning, so we walked part of the way together. As we crossed at the lights, her hand brushed mine. An electric shock passed through me. I apologised and put my hand in my raincoat pocket to prevent another such occurrence. She took off her Sony headset and invited me to listen to her Guns 'n' Roses tape. After five minutes I handed it back to her. I couldn't stand the din.

Tuesday   May 7th

Bianca was there again outside the house this morning. I don't know why she keeps coming down this road. It's not on her route to work.

  Babysat. The kids went to bed at 9.30 p.m., after I'd read them the first three chapters of *Lo!* For once, they seemed quite tired, yawning, etc.

Wednesday   May 8th

Bianca there yet again, tying the laces on her Docs. She told me that she gets bored in the evenings – she hasn't got that many friends in Oxford. She misses the cinema especially, but she is fed up with going on her own. She went on and on about Al Pacino. She has seen *Sea of Love* eleven times. I haven't seen it once. Personally, I can't stand the man. I told her that I too haven't seen a film in ages. When she left me and went into the newsagent's, she looked irritable. Pre-menstrual, probably.

Thursday   May 9th

Babysat. At 7.30 p.m. I offered to read more of *Lo!* to the kids, but they said, as one, that they were very tired and wanted to go to bed! I had a peaceful night washing my working wardrobe and shampooing my beard. Christian got back at 1 a.m. after observing a fight in an Indian restaurant. I advised him to put his trousers in cold water to soak overnight. Turmeric is one of the most stubborn stains known to man. It is a pig to shift once it has gained a hold.

Monday   May 13th

A terrible scandal at lunchtime today! Megan Harris and Bill Blane were caught in the act of photocopying their private parts! They would have got away with it, had the machine not jammed. They have both been suspended on full pay, pending an internal enquiry. I am quite pleased. It has saved me from having to photocopy two hundred pages of Newport Pagnell newt drivel.

Tuesday   May 14th

It is totally unfair. Because of Bill's suspension, I have been given responsibility for the entire Badger Department. Brown threw the badger case histories on my desk and said, 'You're a friend of Bill's. Sort this out.'

Just because Brown was the one to force the photocopy room door open yesterday, there's no need to take it out on me. He may have lost a mistress and a secretary, but he must remember what he learned on his managerial training course and keep his head.

Wednesday   May 15th

Up at dawn to catch taxi to badger set. I must learn to drive. On the return journey, the taxi driver kept complaining about the smell. I had the fresh badger droppings in a sealed D.O.E. jar, so how the aroma came in contact with the taxi driver's nose is a mystery to me. Personally, I found the fresh air 'pine tree' hanging from the roof of his taxi to be much more olfactorily offensive.

Friday   May 17th

I am already up to my ears in newts and badgers, and now Brown is hinting that I may also be given responsibility for *natterjack toads*! He is obviously trying to force me into resigning or having a nervous breakdown due to overwork.

Photocopies of Megan's and Bill's private parts are being passed around the office. I think this is absolutely disgusting – a total invasion of their private lives, not to mention their private parts. Anyway the copies are so blurred that it is impossible to tell which is Bill's and which is Megan's. That photocopier never did work properly.

Bianca came round with Palmer's newspaper bill tonight. I answered the door and would have invited her in, but I didn't want her to think that sexual intercourse was on my mind – though, of course, it was. It's never off my mind. She had obviously gone to some trouble with her clothes, for a change. She was wearing tight denim jeans, high-heeled ankle boots and a white shirt which was tucked into a brown leather belt. She had recently washed her hair. I could smell Wash 'n' Go – the shampoo I use myself. It was on the tip of my tongue to ask her if she would come in for coffee, but something held me back.

She didn't seem to want to move off the doorstep – she kept talking about how fed up she was with having nothing to do in the evening. I was forced to stand in a cold wind, wearing only a shirt and trousers. This could result in a severe chill. I must check my temperature over the next few days.

Sunday   May 19th

As predicted, I woke up on Saturday feeling feverish, so I had three tablespoons of Night Nurse (though it was only 8.30 in the morning) and went back to sleep. On Sunday, Christian knocked on my door at 12.30 p.m. and asked if I could watch the kids for three hours while he attended a 'Stag Strip' at a

Working Men's Club. I reluctantly agreed and dragged myself out of bed.

I myself, personally, have never watched a strip show. I wouldn't know how to arrange my facial features. Would I watch with studied indifference like TV detectives when they are forced to interview scumbag low-life in strip joints? Would I smile and laugh as though *amused* by the sight of a young woman taking her clothes off? Or would I swallow frequently, pant and goggle my eyes and reveal to onlookers that I am sexually excited? I fear the latter.

When Christian returned, he went upstairs. The shower was running for at least three quarters of an hour. I suspect he was symbolically cleansing himself.

Today was an Oombagoomba day, so I didn't – indeed, *couldn't* – talk to the kids.

The Chancellor, Norman Lamont, is going to sue a sex therapist for damages. But *how* did she damage you, Lamont? The British people should be told.

A letter from *Reader's Digest* arrived on Saturday, informing me that my name has been shortlisted out of many hundreds of thousands to receive a huge cash prize! All I have to do is agree to subscribe to the *Reader's Digest* magazine! It is easy to sneer at *Reader's Digest*, but it has to be said that they are an extremely handy way for busy bibliophiles to keep abreast of matters literary.

Plumbs have also written to me, offering to supply a lace circular tablecloth, plus a plywood circular table, should I not already have one. I must say I was quite tempted by both.

Thursday   May 23rd

Christian held a drinks party last night and Cavendish and Pandora came round. I tried to engage Pan in conversation, but every time I did, I could see her eyes looking past me over my shoulder. Am I such boring company?

At 8 o'clock, Bianca turned up in a shiny, tight black dress. I introduced her to Pandora. Pandora said to her, 'That's a great dress, Bianca. God, don't you love lycra? What did we do without it?' They then yakked on about lycra for half an hour. In my opinion, Pandora's expensive education has been entirely wasted.

There must have been at least fifty people in the living-room/kitchen/study at one point. The majority of them were graduates, but you would never have known it from their conversation. The main topics were, in order:

1) *The Archers*
2) Football (Gazza)
3) Lycra
4) University cuts
5) Princess Diana
6) Alcoholism
7) The Oxford murder
8) Oats
9) Rajiv Gandhi being burnt
10) The Gossard Wonderbra

Call themselves intellectuals! My efforts to talk about my book, *Lo! The Flat Hills of My Homeland*, were met with cool indifference. Yes! The so-called 'best brains' in the land listened to me for a few minutes, then made feeble excuses to leave my company. At one point, just as I was telling him about my hero's apprenticeship to a cobbler in Chapter Eleven, a man called Professor Goodchild moved away, saying: 'Please spare me the sodding details.'

Yet only minutes later, I overheard him talking about his fish tank and how best to clean it.

Bianca left at 11.30 in the company of a dubious-looking type in a black leather jacket. He is something big in astrophysics, apparently, though in my opinion he looked like the type of moron who wouldn't know which end of a telescope to put his eye to.

As we were cleaning up after the party, Christian said, 'Adrian, take a tip from me, throw that bloody blazer away. Buy yourself some fashionable, young man's clothes!'

I replied (quite wittily, I thought), 'Lycra doesn't suit me.' He looked puzzled for a moment, then continued to wash the glasses.

Pandora also commented unfavourably, saying, 'That fucking awful blazer: give it to Oxfam, for Christ's sake.'

Perhaps I will.

I lay awake for hours imagining Bianca and the astrophysicist gazing at the stars together. Would he trust her with his telescope?

Friday   May 24th

A household on my route to work has acquired an American pit bull terrier. On the surface, it seems to be a friendly beast. All it does is stand and grin through the fence. But in future I will take a different route to work. This is a considerable inconvenience to me, but I cannot risk facial disfigurement. I would like the photograph on the back of the jacket of my book to show my face as it is today, not hideously scarred. I know that plastic surgeons can work miracles, but from now on I am taking no chances.

Brown was in a foul mood today. He has had a letter from Megan's solicitor. She is threatening to sue him for defamation of character, unless she is reinstated immediately. I hope Brown caves in. Megan's replacement, Ms Julia Stone, is one of those superior types who never lose their money in chocolate machines in railway stations.

Saturday   May 25th

Oxford is full of sightseers riding on the top deck of the tourist buses and walking along the streets gazing upwards. It is extremely annoying to us residents to be asked the way by foreigners every five minutes. Perhaps it is petty of me, but I quite enjoy sending them in the wrong direction.

I have just remembered! When I gave my blazer to the Oxfam shop yesterday, my condom was in the top pocket. This means that, should a sexual opportunity arise today, I will be unprepared. It also means that I can no longer go into the Oxfam shop – at least, not until Mrs Whitlow, the volunteer helper I gave it to, dies or retires. Mrs Whitlow has often congratulated me on being a 'decent, clean-living young man', though I have given her absolutely no grounds for thinking so.

Monday   May 27th

Why do the banks have to close just because it is a Bank Holiday? It is a day when people want to *spend* money, isn't it? Borrowed £5 from Christian for Durex and bananas.

Tuesday   May 28th

I have just finished Chapter Twelve of *Lo! The Flat Hills of My Homeland*, 'The Dog It Had To Die':

> He closed the front door of his mother's house with a sigh. He had left her slumped on the kitchen table surrounded by brimming ashtrays and empty Pilsner cans. Upstairs, his father was injecting heroin into his collapsed veins. The family pet, an American pit bull terrier, looked out from the front window of the squalid terraced house and growled, showing its fearsome jaws. He walked down the street and tossed off greetings to the stunted neighbours. A couple fornicated in an alley, their eyes dead, their motions automatic. He wept internally. Anguish gripped his soul. He rued the day he had been born. Then, suddenly, a shaft of sunlight fell across his path. He stood, mesmerised. Was it a sign, a portent, that his life would improve from now?
>
> He turned and went back to the house. He opened the front door. The dog, Butcher, growled at him, so he strangled it until the dog lay dead at his feet. He felt Evil, but at the same time strangely Good. The dog had been nothing but a nuisance and nobody ever took it for a walk. His conscience was clear.

Wow! Powerful writing, or what? I believe Dostoievsky would be proud of me. Canine murder is surely a first in English fiction. I expect I'll get a few letters from English dog lovers when *Lo! The Flat Hills of My Homeland* is published, but I shall write back and point out that I am an artist and must go where my pen takes me.

Wednesday   May 29th

Julia Stone and I had a brief conversation at the Autovent machine today, while my oxtail soup was pouring into my plastic cup. She asked me not to use the ladies' lavatory again. I pointed out to her that the men's lavatory had run out of toilet paper, but she said if I continued to 'invade female space', she would report me for sexual harassment. She also said that she had checked the post book and that I used more postage stamps than any other member of staff.

I told her in cold tones – though not as cold as my oxtail soup – that I wrote more letters, therefore I needed more stamps. But I fear I have made an enemy.

Ms Julia Stone is a daunting woman. My throat constricts whenever I have to talk to her. Lipstick might help. Her, not me.

Christian returned from the Golden Gate nightclub with a black eye. His crime was to look at a yob. Yes, the yob accused Christian of 'looking' at him. This is a frightening example of the disintegration of British society. Yobs used to *enjoy* people looking at them. From now on, I shall avert my eyes whenever I see a yobbish person approaching me.

After Christian had stopped fussing with his eye and gone to bed, I sat at the kitchen table and tried to get some sex into *Lo! The Flat Hills of My Homeland*.

> *Chapter Thirteen: Deflowering*
> He lay in bed in his Parisian bedroom. Fifi began to
> remove her lycra dress. His breathing rate increased.
> She stood revealed before him, her chest strained beneath
> her Gossard Wonderbra, her knickers were clean and nicely
> ironed. He reached out for her, but she said to him in her
> French accent, 'No, no, *mon amour*, I am thinking you must
> wait.' His ardour increased as he noticed that her bottom
> was smooth and had no pimples. He groaned and . . .

It's no good. I can't write about sex. Not even French sex in Paris.

Saturday June 1st

Two letters, one from Plumbs, offering me a set of matching towels with my personal monogram embroidered on the hems; the other from Sharon Bott.

> Dear Adrian,
> I hope you are well   long time no see   I saw your mum
> in town and we had a talk   she said how much Glenn
> looked like you   I said yes and she said is he our Adrians
> Sharon I must know   she just came out with it like that   I

din't know what to say   I have got to confess I was seeing someone else at the time as I was seeing you I din't want to double time you Adrian but you was sometimes moody and I wanted some laffs I was only young. Glenn is going to school now and is a big boy. My mum says you should pay some money but I said no mum it would not be fair cause I dont no if Glenn is Adrians or not   Your mum gave me this address to write to you   I hope they're is not to many spelling mistakes and that but I never write anything now since I left school their is no need I saw Baz on the telly did you   He has done alright for himself I have not got a bloke now sinse Daryl run off with the video and £35 I had saved for the gas   I have put a bit of wait on but I am going to go to Waitwatchers and get it off   You mum said she would babysit   she is so good to me.

Cheers,
Sharon

Sunday   June 2nd

I spoke to my mother this morning and ordered her to keep her nose out of my affairs. She said, 'Glenn is the *result* of one of your affairs,' and put the phone down. From then on, I got the engaged signal.

I was enraged by my mother's interference. How dare *she* pontificate about *anybody*'s morals? I know for a fact that she was not a virgin on her wedding night. Grandma told me.

And anyway, my mother should not have spoken in the plural. I have not had *affairs*. I have had *an* affair. In the singular. With Sharon Bott, a simpleton who cannot differentiate between 'they're', 'there' and 'their' and is a virtual stranger to the comma and full stop. She probably thinks that a semi-colon is a partial removal of the intestines.

Memo to self: Is the kid mine? Blood test? Letter of denial?

2 a.m. Wrote to Sharon.

3 a.m. Destroyed the letter. (My reply to her must be carefully crafted. I need time to read up on the law relating to paternity.)

Tuesday June 4th

Thank God, Prince William has made a full recovery after being bashed on the head by a golf club. When I think how close we came to losing our future King, my heart stands still. Well, not literally *still*, it doesn't *stop*, but I'm glad the kid is better. I phoned Grandma in Leicester. She wanted to know why Prince Charles didn't pick his son up from the hospital. She said, 'Doesn't he know that it is traditional in our English culture?' She thinks that the monarchy is losing touch with the common herd and she complained bitterly that the Royal Yacht *Britannia* costs thirty-five thousand pounds a week to run.

5.00 p.m. The *Oxford Mail* has just informed me that the emir of Kuwait has yet to announce the date for democratic elections to be held in his country. Puzzling, considering all the trouble and expense the allies went to only recently. Get a move on, emir! I'm also informed by the *Oxford Mail* that the Royal Yacht *Britannia* costs thirty-five thousand pounds *a day*! *A day*! I phoned Grandma immediately and put her right. She was disgusted.

Query: Why does the emir of Kuwait spell his name with a small 'e'?

Friday June 7th

I spent the morning writing a report on a projection of newt births and the early afternoon on a report on the distribution of badgers. But I fear some of the paperwork has got mixed up. As I was photocopying the reports, I noticed that I had muddled a few facts. However, Brown was shouting down the corridor for the reports, so what could I do? His management meeting was due to start at 4 p.m., so I had no choice but to hand him the papers.

Saturday June 8th

Wrote to Sharon:

Dear Sharon,

How very nice to hear from you after all this time.

I'm afraid that there is no chance at all that I can be the father of your child, Glenn.

I have recently had my sperm counted and I was informed by the Consultant Spermatologist that my sperms are too weak to transform themselves into a child. This is a personal tragedy to me, as I had planned on having at least six children.

You mention in your letter that you were double-timing me. I was most upset to read this – our relationship was not ideal, I know; we came from different backgrounds: me: upper working/lower middle; you: lower working/underclass. And, of course, our educational attainments are worlds apart, not to mention our cultural interests. But despite these differences, I had thought that we rubbed along quite well sexually. I see absolutely no reason why you should have betrayed me and sought out another sexual partner. I confess that I am devastated by your revelation. I feel cheap and used. I would be most obliged to you if you would stop seeing my mother. She is addicted to human dramas of any kind. She thinks of herself as a character in a soap opera. I suggest that you should go to Weight-watchers (not *Wait*watchers, by the way), and hire yourself a competent child-minder. My mother is not to be trusted with young children: she dropped me on my head at the age of six months, whilst taking a boiled egg out of a saucepan.

Anyway, Sharon, it was very nice to hear from you.

Regards,

Adrian

P.S. Who were you double-timing me with? Not that it matters, of course. I have had a constant stream of lovers since our relationship ended. It is simple curiosity on my part. But I would like to know the youth's name, though it is not in the least important. Don't feel obliged to let me know. I just think it may help you to get it off your chest. Guilt can eat away at you, can't it? So would you please write to me and let me know the youth's name? I think you would feel better about yourself.

Sunday   June 9th

I spent the day quietly, working on Chapter Fourteen of my novel.

> He looked at the young boy, who was poking a stick at a natterjack toad. 'Stop!' he cried. 'It is one of an endangered species. You must be kind to it.' The young child stopped poking at the toad and came to hold his hand.
>
> 'Who are you?' lisped the child. He longed to shout, 'I am your *father*, boy!' but it was impossible. He looked at Sharon Slagg, the boy's mother, who weighed twenty-one stone and had numerous split ends. How could he have once enjoyed sexual congress with her?
>
> He let go of the boy's hand and said, 'I am nobody, boy. I am a stranger to you. I am simply a person who loves the planet we live on – including the dumb creatures that we share our planet with.'
>
> With that, he walked away from his son. The boy exclaimed, 'Please, stranger, don't go.' But he knew he must, before Sharon Slagg looked up from *Damage*, the book she was reading on the park bench. The boy said, 'I wish you were my father, stranger, then I too would have a daddy to come to parents' evenings.'
>
> He thought his heart would break. Sobbingly, he walked away across the grass until the boy was the size of an ant in the distance.

I don't mind admitting that this piece of writing had me wiping my eyes. God, I'm clever. I can tug at the heart strings like no other writer I know. I do feel that my book is now vastly improved by these additions. It still lacks narrative thrust (or does it?), but nobody can say that it doesn't engage the reader's emotions.

Thursday June 20th

Bianca came round tonight to borrow a cup of Basmati rice. She has stopped going out with the Stargazer: she said his breath smelled constantly of kiwi fruit.

She is a nicely spoken girl, with quite an extensive vocabulary. I asked her why she was serving in a newsagent's. She said, 'There are no jobs for qualified engineers.'

I was totally gobsmacked to learn that Bianca has an upper second degree in Hydraulic Engineering – from Edinburgh University. Before she left with the rice, I asked her to mend the leaking shower in my room. She said she would be pleased to come round tomorrow night and see to it for me. She asked if she should bring a bottle of wine with her. I said there was no need. She looked disappointed. I sincerely hope she is not an alcoholic or a heavy drinker who needs a 'nip' before she can do a job of work.

I am making good progress on the novel. I took out my epic poem *The Restless Tadpole* tonight. It is amazingly good, but I can't spare the time to finish it. The novel has to come first. There is no money in poetry. Our Poet Laureate, Ted Hughes, has been wearing the same jacket in his photograph for the past twenty years.

Friday June 21st

Bianca came round *avec* tool box, but *sans* wine. She hung about after she'd fixed the shower and talked about how lonely she is and how she longs to have a regular boy friend. She asked me if I have a regular girl friend. I replied in the negative. I sat in the armchair under the window and she lay on my bed in what an old-fashioned kind of man could have interpreted as a provocative pose.

I wanted to join her on the bed, but I wasn't sure how she would react. Would she welcome me with open arms and legs? Or would she run downstairs screaming and ask Christian to call the police? Women are a complete mystery to me. One minute they are flapping their eyelashes, the next they are calling you a sexist pig.

While I tried to work it out, a silence fell between us, so I

started to talk about the revisions I am making to my book.
After about twenty minutes, she fell into a deep sleep. It was
a most awkward situation to be in.

Eventually, I went downstairs and asked Christian to come
and wake her up. He sneered and said, 'You're unbelievably
stupid at times.' What did he mean? Was he referring to my
inability to fix my own shower head, or to my timidity regarding
sex?

When Bianca woke up she looked like a sad child. I
wanted to put my arms round her but before I could she had
grabbed her tool box and run down the stairs without saying
goodnight.

Saturday   June 22nd

Had a most satisfactory shower this morning. The force
of the water has improved considerably.

2.00 p.m. Worked on Chapter Fifteen. I have sent *him* to
China.

11.30 p.m. I have brought *him* back from China. Can't
be bothered to do all that tedious research. I just got
him walking along the Great Wall, then flying back to East
Midlands Airport. I went down to the kitchen to make myself
a cup of hot chocolate and told Christian about my hero's trip
to China. Christian said, 'But you told me that he is a pauper.
Where would he get the money for his air ticket?' God, how I hate
pedants!

1.00 a.m. Insert for Chapter Fifteen:

> What was this on the mat? He bent down and picked
> up a letter from the *Reader's Digest*. On the front of
> the expensively papered envelope was written 'OPEN AT
> ONCE'. He obeyed. Inside was a letter and a cheque for
> one million pounds! He was fabulously rich! 'How shall I
> spend it all?' he asked the cat. The female cat looked back
> at him inscrutably. 'China?' he said. 'I'll have a day trip to
> China!'

I hope this satisfies my pedantic landlord and my most critical of readers.

Sunday   June 23rd

At breakfast, I told Christian how my hero got the money to go to China. He now wants to know what my hero does with the *remaining* money. There is no pleasing him.

12 noon

> *Chapter Sixteen: A Gratuitous Act*
> The beggar outside Leicester bus station stared in disbelief as £999,000 showered down onto his head. *He* walked away, a pauper once again.

5.00 p.m. Saw Bianca walking towards me as I was returning from my perambulations around the Outer Ring Road this afternoon. She was wearing shorts and a tee shirt: her legs, apart from the ankles, looked superb, long and slim. I hurried towards her. To my astonishment, she crossed over the road and ignored me. So much for Christian telling me that she fancies me! It's certainly a good job I didn't join her on the bed the other night. I could be in prison now, on a sexual assault charge.

The next time I go to the library I will try to find a book that explains to the intelligent layman how women's brains work.

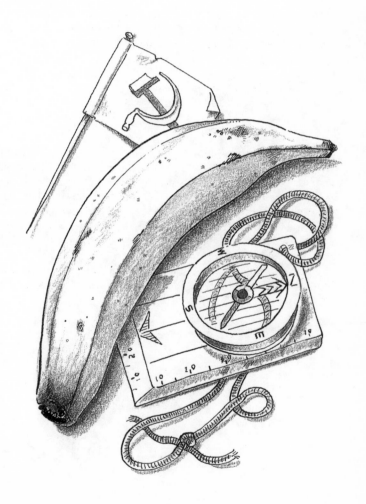

Wednesday   July 3rd

Brown reminded me today that I have two weeks' holiday entitlement which I will lose unless I take it within the next two months.

Rang my travel agent. Told her I want two weeks in Europe in a four star hotel with half board, but for no more than £300. She promised to ring back if anything turned up in Albania. I said, 'Not Albania, I hear the food is inaudible.' After I'd put the phone down, I remembered that the word for bad food is, of course, 'inedible'. I hope I'm not suffering from an early onset of senile dementia. Word-loss is an early signal.

Friday   July 5th

The travel agent rang today. Unfortunately, the call was put through to Brown's office, where I was being reprimanded because of a mix-up over the newt and badger reports. The Department of Transport had received the erroneous intelligence that a family of badgers had appeared on the route of the projected Newport Pagnell bypass. Naturally, I was constrained by Brown's presence, so I was unable to concentrate on what the travel agent was saying.

I said that I would ring her back, but she said, 'You must book it *now* if you want it.'

I said, 'Book what?'

She said, 'Your holiday. A week on the Russian lakes and rivers, and a week in Moscow. A fortnight for £299.99, full board.'

'Go ahead,' I said.

Saturday   July 6th

Rang 'Easy-pass' Driving School and booked a free lesson as advertised in the *Oxford Mail*. I take to the road on Thursday, July 18th.

I have taken driving lessons before, but have been badly let down by my previous instructors. They were all incompetent.

Sunday   July 7th

Babysat while Christian went to bingo. He won £7.50 and was near to winning the area prize of £14,000. He only needed two fat ladies.

Monday   July 8th

Worked on *Lo!* Shall I give *him* a name? If so, what shall it be? It needs to express his sensitivity, his courage, his individualism, his intellectual vigour, his success with women, his affinity with nature, his proletarian roots.

Tuesday   July 9th

How about Jake Westmorland?

Wednesday   July 10th

Maurice Pritchard?

Thursday   July 11th

Oscar Brimmington?

Friday   July 12th

Jake Pritchard?

Saturday   July 13th

Maurice Brimmington?

Sunday   July 14th

A decision will have to be made soon. I can't move on with my book until it has. Christian prefers 'Jake Westmorland'. However, the man in the greengrocer's likes the sound of 'Oscar Brimmington'. Whereas a bus conductor, whose opinion I sought, was very keen on 'Maurice Westmorland'.

Monday   July 15th

Spent the day babysitting. I got the kids to test me on the Highway Code. Somebody kept ringing the house tonight. A woman. All she said was, 'Hello.' But when I asked who was calling she put the phone down. It sounded like Bianca, but why should she behave in such a childish manner?

Tuesday   July 16th

Brown had to have his surgical corset adjusted at the Radcliffe Hospital this morning, so I took the opportunity to go into his office and look at my file: 'MOLE – ADRIAN.'

> FORESIGHT – NONE
> PUNCTUALITY – POOR
> INITIATIVE – NONE
> RELIABILITY – QUITE GOOD
> HONESTY – SUSPECTED OF PILFERING POST-
> AGE STAMPS
> ACCEPTANCE OF RESPONSIBILITY – POOR
> RELATIONS WITH OTHERS – QUITE GOOD
> I believe his 'A' level Biology qualification to be bogus.

Wednesday   July 17th

> Dear Mr Brown,
> It is with great regret that I write to inform you of my intention to resign from the Department of the Environment. I will of course serve out my statutory two months' notice. I have been unhappy for some time now with how the department is run. I feel that my talents have been

wasted. Collecting badger faeces was not in my original job description.

Also, in my opinion, the protection of animals has reached ludicrous levels. The beasts have more rights than I do. Take bats. If I were to hang upside down and defecate in a church, I would be taken away to an institution. Yet bats are *encouraged* by conservationists such as yourself, Mr Brown. It's no wonder that our churches are empty of parishioners.

I remain, sir,

Adrian Mole

At 10.00 a.m. I wrote the above letter, put it into an envelope and wrote 'FOR THE ATTENTION OF MR BROWN'.

At 11.00 a.m., after staring down at the envelope for a full hour, I put it under my blotting pad. Thinking perhaps that I could brazen it out regarding the bogus 'A' level.

At midday, while I was at the Autovent, the envelope disappeared. I searched my cubicle but found nothing, apart from my little blue comb.

At 1.00 p.m., I was summoned to Brown's office and told to clear my desk and leave the premises immediately. He gave me an envelope which contained a cheque for £676.31 = two months' pay plus holiday money less tax and National Insurance.

Who delivered my resignation letter? I suspect the Sexually Harassed One.

So, like three and a half million of my fellow citizens, I am without work.

1 a.m. Christian got me drunk tonight. I had two and a half glasses of Vouvray and a pint of draught Guinness in a can.

Thursday   July 18th

DRIVING LESSON

Stayed in bed until 2 p.m. My driving instructor is a woman called Fiona. She is old (47) and has got lots of loose skin around her neck, which she pulls at in times of crisis. I did *tell* her that it is over a year since I was behind the wheel. I did *ask* if I could practise first on Tesco's Megastore out-of-town car park, but Fiona refused and forced me to drive on real roads with real traffic. So what happened at the roundabout was not my fault. Fiona should have been quicker with the dual controls.

Friday July 19th

A letter from Faber and Faber:

> Dear Mr Mole,
> I am afraid that I am returning your manuscript, *Lo! The Flat Hills of My Homeland.*
> It is a most amusing parody of the English *naïf* school of fiction.
> However, we do not have a place for such a book on our list at the moment.
> Yours sincerely,
>
> Matthew Evans

After reading the letter six times, I tore it in pieces. Mr Evans will be sorry one day. When my work is being auctioned in hotel rooms, I will instruct my agent to disqualify Mr Evans from the bidding.

There was no reason to get up, so I stayed in bed all day, wondering if there was any point in going on. Pandora despises me, I am out of work and I am incapable of driving a car in a straight line. At 7 p.m. I got out of my bed and rang Leonora. A man answered the phone: 'De Witt.'

'It's Adrian Mole,' I said. 'Could I speak to Leonora?'

'My wife's dressing,' he said; which threw me for a while. Images of Leonora in various lingerie outfits flashed into my mind.

'It's an emergency,' I managed to croak out. I heard him put the receiver down with a crack and shout, 'Darling, it's for you. Something about moles.'

There was a muttered oath, and then Leonora came on the phone.

'Yes?'

'Leonora, I'm in despair. Can I come round and see you?'

'When?'

'Now.'

'No, I'm giving a dinner party at eight and the first course is an asparagus soufflé.'

I wondered why she would think I was remotely interested in her menu.

'I need to talk to you,' I said. 'I've lost my job, my novel's been rejected and I crashed the driving school car yesterday.'

'They are all life experiences,' she said. 'You will come out of this a stronger man.'

I heard her husband shouting something in the background. Then she said, 'I have to go. Why don't you talk to that girl, Bianca? Goodbye.'

I did as I was told. I went and stood outside Bianca's house and looked up at her flat. Nobody went in or came out.

After watching for an hour I went home and got back into bed. I hope the De Witts and their guests all choked on their asparagus soufflé.

Saturday July 20th

Cassandra Palmer turned up on the doorstep this afternoon. Christian's face turned white when he saw his wife. The children greeted her politely, but without much enthusiasm, I noticed. She looks as though she wrestles in mud for a living. I loathed her on sight. I cannot stand big women who shave their heads. I prefer them with hair.

Her first words to me were, 'Oh, so *you*'re the cuckoo in the nest.'

Sunday July 21st

The dictatorship of Cassandra started this morning. Our household is not allowed to drink tap water, coffee, tea or alcohol, nor to eat eggs, cheese, chocolate, fruit yoghurt, Marks and Spencer's lemon slices ... etc., etc. The list goes on forever. There are also things we mustn't say. I happened to mention that Bianca's boss, the newsagent, is a fat man. Cassandra snapped, 'He's not fat, he's dimensionally challenged.'

I laughed, thinking this was a good joke, but Cassandra's mouth turned into a grim slit and with horror I realised she was serious.

Christian remarked to his wife over lunch that he was losing his hair, 'going bald' were his words. Once again, Cassandra snapped into action.

'You're a little follicularly disadvantaged, that's all,' she said, as she inspected the top of her husband's head.

I cannot share this house with that woman, or *her* language. It is not as though she is pleasant to look at. She is as ugly as sin, or, as she might put it, she is facially impaired.

Monday   July 22nd

I asked Bianca if she would keep a lookout for suitable accommodation. She agreed, though there is nothing to keep me here in Oxford any more, apart from my unrequited love for Dr Pandora Braithwaite.

Tuesday   July 23rd

> *Dr Braithwaite*
> Since you gained your Ph.D.
> You have had no time for me.
> You loved me once, you could again.
> Pandora, give up other men!
> You swore to love me for all time.
> As long as Moon and June would rhyme.
> Please marry me and be my wife.
> For you I'll sacrifice my life.
> I'll stay at home, I'll cook and clean
> In the background, never seen.
> When you return from brainy toil,
> I'll have the kettle on the boil.
> While you translate from Serbo-Croat,
> I will shake our coco doormat.
> I'll gladly wash your duvet cover,
> If only I can be your lover.

I put the poem through Pandora's door at 4 a.m. This is my last-ditch attempt to sound out Pandora's true feelings for me. Leonora has said that I must move on emotionally. What will Pandora's reaction be?

Wednesday   July 24th

I found this letter on the doormat.

> Dear Adrian,
> You woke me at 4 a.m. with your clumsy manipulation
> of my letter box. Your poem caused my lover and me
> much merriment. I hope, for your sake, that it was *meant*
> to be funny. If it was *not*, then I urge you to seek further
> psychiatric advice from Leonora. She told me that you have
> stopped seeing her regularly. Is it the cost?
>   I *know* you can afford £30 a week. You don't drink,
> or smoke, or wear decent clothes. You cut your own hair,
> you don't run a car. You don't gamble or take drugs. You
> live rent-free. Withdraw some money from your precious
> Building Society and *get help*.
>   Regards,
>   Pandora
>
> P.S. Incidentally, I am *not* a Ph.D., as you state in your
> poem. I am a D.Phil. A subtle but important difference
> here in Oxford.

So that's it. If Pandora came to me tomorrow, begging to be
Mrs A. A. Mole, I would have to turn her down. I have moved
on. It's Leonora I must see. Must.

Thursday   July 25th

5.15 p.m. I have just phoned Leonora and insisted that she
gives me an emergency appointment. I said I had something
momentous to tell her. She agreed reluctantly.

9.30 p.m. I burst into Leonora's room this evening and found
her with another client, a middle-aged man who was sobbing
into a Kleenex (woman trouble, I suppose). I was ten minutes
early and Leonora was furious and ordered me to wait outside.
At 6.30 p.m. precisely, I knocked on her door and she shouted,
'Come.' She was still in a bad mood and so I tried to make conversation and asked her what had upset the sobbing middle-aged
man. This angered her even more. 'What is said to me in this room

remains confidential,' she said. 'How would *you* feel if I talked about *your* problems to my other clients?'

'I don't like to think about you having other clients,' I confessed.

She sighed deeply and curled a hank of black hair around her finger. 'So what's the momentous happening?' she said eventually.

'I've moved on from Pandora Braithwaite,' I said, and I told her about the poem and Pandora's reaction to it and my reaction to Pandora's reaction. At that moment, a tall, dark man wearing a suede shirt came in. He looked surprised to see me.

'Sorry, darling. I can't find the small grater, for the parmesan.'

'Second drawer down, darling, next to the Aga,' she said, looking up at him in rapt adoration.

'Terribly sorry,' he said.

When he'd gone out, I stood up and said, 'How dare your husband interrupt my consultation with his petty domestic enquiries?'

Leonora said, 'My husband didn't know you were here. I squeezed you in, if you remember.' Her tone was carefully measured, but I noticed that a vein was pulsating on the side of her temple and that she was wringing her hands.

'You should learn to express your anger, Leonora. It's no good for you to bottle it up,' I said.

She then said, 'Mr Mole, you are not making progress with me. I suggest you try another analyst.'

'No,' I said. 'It's you I want to see. You're my reason for living.'

'So,' she said. 'Think what you're saying. Are you saying that without me you would commit suicide?'

I hesitated. Noises of pans banging and glasses tinkling came up from the basement, as did a delicious smell that made my mouth water. For some reason I blurted out, 'Could I stay to dinner?'

'No. I never socialise with my clients,' she said, looking at her slim, gold watch.

I sat down and asked, 'How mad am I, on a scale of one to ten?'

'You're not mad at all,' she said. 'As Freud said, "It is impossible for a therapist to treat either the mad or those in love."'

'But I *am* in love. With you,' I added.

Leonora sighed very deeply. Her breasts rose and fell under her embroidered sweater.

'That is why I think that seeing another therapist would be a good idea. I have a friend, Reinhard Kowolski, who has a superb reputation . . .'

I didn't wait to hear any more about Herr Kowolski. I left her room and put three ten pound notes on the hall table, next to the laughing Buddha and walked out into the street.

I felt angry, so I decided to express my anger and I kicked an empty Diet Coke can all the way home.

When I got to the attic, I laid out all my job-searching clothes ready for the morning. Then I lay on my bed with the *Oxford Mail* and ringed all the likely looking jobs in the situations vacant columns.

There was nothing that required one 'A' level in English.

Friday July 26th

Went to the Job Centre, but the queue was too long, so returned to find Cassandra in the kitchen, examining the children's books, pen in hand. She picked one up and changed *Winnie the Pooh* to *Winnie the Shit*. 'I hate ambiguity,' she explained, as she snapped the cap back on her Magic Marker.

Saturday July 27th

Saw Brown in W. H. Smith's, buying the current wildlife magazines. He smiled and said, 'Enjoying your life of leisure, Mole?'

I forced a smile to my lips and said, 'On the contrary, Brown, I am working as hard as ever. I am a middle manager at the Book Trust in Cambridge, at £25,000 a year, plus car. I got the position thanks to my having English Literature at 'A' level.' Brown stormed off, forgetting to pay for his magazines. He was stopped on the pavement by a security guard. I didn't hang around to watch Brown's humiliation.

Sunday July 28th

Stayed in room all day, out of Cassandra's way. She is insisting that everyone in the house meditates for half an hour each morning. Christian has stopped doing his research into popular culture. Cassandra objected to the smell of cigarette smoke on his clothes when he returned from his low-class haunts. If she is not careful, she will wreck his academic career.

I am living on my savings, but I cannot continue to do so. The State will have to keep me – after all, I didn't ask to be born, did I? And one day the State will be glad it supported me. When I am a high-rate taxpayer.

However, before I throw myself on its mercy, I am going to tramp the streets of Oxford tomorrow and look for a job, any job that doesn't involve driving or working with animals.

Next year, I will have lived for a quarter of a century and as yet I have made no mark on the world – apart from winning a *Leicester Mercury* literary prize when I was seventeen.

If I died tomorrow, what would be written on my tomb-stone?

> Adrian Albert Mole
> Unpublished novelist
> and pedestrian

> Mourned by few
> Scorned by many
> Winner of the *Leicester Mercury*
> 'Clean Up Leicester' Essay Prize

Tuesday   July 30th

Why do beggars *always* want money for a cup of tea? Don't any of them drink coffee?

Wednesday   July 31st

Why didn't palace flunkies arrange for Princess Diana to be kept dry at the open-air Pavarotti concert last night? If she develops pneumonia and dies, the country will be plunged into crisis and Charles will be devastated with grief. He obviously adores her. Somebody's head should roll.

Thursday   August 1st

Dear Adrian,
I was sorry to read about your poor cwallity seed   the
person I was seeing on the side was barry kent   I feel
better now it is off my chest.
Yours sinserely,
Sharon

Barry Kent! I should have known! He is an amoral, talentless
turd! He is lower than a cesspit. He has the prose style of a *Daily
Sport* leader writer. He wouldn't know what a semi-colon was if
it fell into his beer. The little I have read of *Dork's Diary* forced
me to the conclusion that Kent should be arrested and charged
with criminal assault on the English language. He deserves to
burn in everlasting hell with a catherine wheel tied to his cheating
penis.

Friday   August 2nd

Dear Sharon,
Many thanks for your commiserations regarding my 'seed',
as you put it. May I suggest that you get in touch with Barry
Kent (who, as you know, is now both *rich* and famous) and
ask him to contribute to Glenn's upbringing? The least
Kent can do is to send Glenn to a private school, thus
giving his child an excellent start in life.
I remain,
Yours,
Adrian

P.S. I am absolutely sure that Barry will be thrilled
to hear that he has a child.
P.P.S. Eton is quite a good private public school.

Sunday   August 4th

Cassandra announced at breakfast that she has taken the
locks off the bathroom and lavatory doors. 'Inhibitions about
nakedness and bodily functions are the reason why the English are no good at sex,' she said. She looked pointedly

at her husband, who blushed and rubbed the side of his nose.

The Queen Mother is 91 today. I suppose she doesn't think it is worth getting her teeth seen to now. I can see her point.

Monday   August 5th

Contacted Foreign Parts, the travel agents, about my Russian cruise and explained that I have been made redundant and would like to cancel and have my money back. The travel agent told me that it was impossible and told me to refer to the small print on my documents. I peered in vain and eventually went to Boots and bought a pair of 'off the peg' reading spectacles for £7.99. The travel agent was right; I will have to go.

Tuesday   August 6th

Christian told me (shamefaced) that Cassandra requires my attic room. She is opening a reincarnation centre where people can get in touch with their former selves. She wants me out of the attic by mid-September. I couldn't help myself. I burst out, 'Your wife is a cow!' Christian said, 'I know, but she used to be a kitten.'

So, no job and, when I get back from the Russian cruise, nowhere to live.

Thursday   August 8th

Dear John Tydeman,
The last time I wrote to you, it was to apologise for clogging up the BBC's fax machines with my 700-page novel, *Lo! The Flat Hills of My Homeland.* You sent it back to me (eventually) and said, and I quote: 'Your manuscript is awash with consonants, but vowels are very thin on the ground, thin to the point of non-existence.'

You will, I am sure, be delighted to hear that I have now reinstated the vowels and have spent this year rewriting the first sixteen chapters, and I would value your comments on them. They are enclosed with this letter. I

know you are busy, but it wouldn't take you long. You can
read them in the BBC's coffee lounge during your coffee
breaks, etc.

I remain, Sir,

Yours,

Adrian Mole

10.30 p.m. I have seen Leonora for the last time. She has
dismissed me from my post as her client. I overplayed my
hand and declared my love for her. In fact, it wasn't so much
a declaration, it was more of a proclamation. It was probably
heard all over Oxford. Her husband heard it because he came
into the room with a tea towel and a little blue jug in his hand
and asked Leonora if she was all right.

'Thank you, Fergus, darling,' she said. 'Mr Mole will
be leaving soon.'

'I'll be outside if you need me,' he said, and left, leaving
the door slightly open.

Leonora said, 'Mr Mole, I am calling a halt to our professional
relationship, but before you leave I would like to reassure you
that your problems are capable of being solved.

'You expect too much of yourself,' she said, leaning forward
sympathetically. 'Let yourself off the hook. Be *kind* to yourself.
You've expressed your worries about world famine, the ozone
layer, homelessness, the Aids epidemic, many times. These are
not only your problems. They are shared by sensitive people all
over the world. You can have no control over these sad situations
– apart from donating money. However, over your personal worries, lack of success with your novel, problems with women, you
do have a certain amount of control.' Here she stopped and she
looked as though she wanted to take my hand, but she didn't.

'You are an attractive, healthy young man,' she said. 'I
have not read your manuscript, so I can't comment on your
literary talent or otherwise, but what I do know is that there
is somebody out there who is going to make you happy.'

I turned on my dining chair and looked out of the window.
'Not literally out there, of course,' she snapped, following my
glance. She stood up, shook my hand and said, 'There will be
no charge for this session.'

I said, 'It isn't transference: it's true love.'

'I've heard that at least twenty times,' she said, softly. She rose to her feet. Her rings sparkled under the light and she shook my hand. As I left, I passed her husband, who was still drying the little blue jug twenty minutes later. A suitable case for treatment if ever I saw one.

'I intend to marry your wife one day,' I said, before closing the front door.

'Yes, that's what they all say. Cheerio.' He smiled and went towards Leonora and I closed the door on a painful – and expensive – period of my life.

Friday   August 9th

> Adrian,
> What the fuck are you playing at, getting Sharon Bott to write to me and ask for money to send her sprog to fucking Eton? I'm down here at Jeanette Winterson's place, trying to finish my second novel and I can do without all this fucking rubbish.
>
> Baz

Saturday   August 10th

I looked in the Job Centre window today. There were three vacancies in the window. One for a 'mobile cleansing operative' (road sweeper?), one for a 'peripatetic catering assistant' (pizza delivery?) and one for a 'part-time clowns enabler' (!). I didn't exactly reach excitedly for the Basildon Bond on my return to Stalag Cassandra.

Sunday   August 11th

Went to the newsagent's. Bianca is back from Greece. She has got a fantastic tan. She was wearing a low-cut white tee shirt, which displayed her breasts. They looked like small, ripe, russet apples. I asked her facetiously if she had had a holiday romance. She laughed and admitted that she had – with a fisherman who had never heard of Chekhov. I asked if she was going to continue the romance. She gave me a strange look and said: 'How would you *feel* about it if I did, Adrian?'

I was about to reply when a member of the underclass thrust a *Sunday Sport* into her hands, so the moment was lost.

10.00 p.m. How do I feel about Bianca's holiday romance? I'm always pleased to see her, but I can't stop comparing her to the lovely Leonora: Bianca is a Malteser: Leonora is an Elizabeth Shaw gold-wrapped after dinner mint.

Tuesday   August 13th

I leave for Russia on Thursday. I bought myself a new toiletry bag – it's time I treated myself. I hope there are some decent women of childbearing age aboard.

I spent the evening packing. I decided not to take any books. I expect there will be a library on the ship, well stocked with the classics of Russian literature in good translations. I hope my fellow passengers are cultured people. It would be intolerable to have to share the dining room and decks with English lager louts. I decided to include a huge bunch of semi-ripe bananas amongst my luggage. I am used to eating a banana a day and I have heard they are in short supply in Russia.

Saturday   August 17th

River camp – Russia

It is 7.30 p.m. There is no cruise ship. There are no passengers. Each member of our party is paddling their own canoe. I am crouched inside a two-man tent. Outside are swarms of huge, black mosquitoes. They are waiting for me to emerge. I can hear the river throwing itself over the rapids. With a bit of luck, I will die in my sleep.

The man I have been sharing my tent with, Leonard Clifton, is out chopping trees down with a machete, borrowed from Boris, one of our river guides. I sincerely hope that one of Clifton's trees falls on his horrible bald head. I cannot stand another night listening to his interminable anecdotes about the Church Army.

I told Boris earlier today that I would give him all my roubles if he would arrange for me to be airlifted to Moscow.

He paused from repairing the hole in my canoe and said, 'But you must paddle now to the river's end, Mister Mole; there is no inhabitations, peoples or telephonings here.'

On my return to civilisation, I will sue Foreign Parts for every penny they've got. At no time did they mention that I would be paddling a canoe, sleeping in a tent, or drinking water from the river. The worst privation of all is that *I have got nothing to read*. Clifton lent me his Bible, but it fell overboard at the last rapids. As I watched it sink, I shouted 'My God, my God, why hast thou forsaken me?' To the bewilderment of the rest of the group and of myself, I must admit.

Monica and Stella Brightways, the twins from Barnstaple, are outside leading the singing of 'Ten Green Bottles'. Leonard and the rest of the gang are joining in lustily.

10.00 p.m. Tent. I have just returned from the forest, where I was forced to urinate into the darkness. I stood with the others round the fire for a moment, drinking black tea.

Monica Brightways had a serious argument with the scout-master from Hull. She claimed she saw him take two slices of black bread from the sack at lunchtime. He denied it vehemently and accused her of hogging the camp fire. Everyone took sides, apart from me, who loathes them both equally.

Capsized eleven times earlier today. The rest of the hearties were furious with me for holding them up. It is all right for them. They are all members of the British Canoe Union. I am a complete novice and crossing a lake in a force-nine gale is something out of my worst nightmare. The Waves! The Wind! The Water! The lowering black Russian sky! The Danger! The Fear!

I pray to God we may soon come to our journey's end. I long for Moscow. Though I will have to stay in my hotel room; the mosquitoes have attacked my face unmercifully. I look like the Elephant Man on acid.

Midnight The drinking of vodka is now taking place. From my tent I can hear every word. The Russians are maudlin. Every time they talk about 'our souls', the English snigger. I crave sleep. I also crave hot water and a flushing lavatory.

Moscow! Moscow! Moscow!

Wednesday   August 21st

Moscow train

The lavatory on the train defies description. However, I'll try. After all, I am a novelist.

Imagine that twenty buffalo with loose bowels have been trapped inside the lavatory for two weeks. Then try to imagine that an open sewer runs across the floor. Add an I.R.A. prisoner on dirty protest. Then concoct a smell by digging up a few decomposed corpses, add a couple of healthy young skunks and you come quite near to what the lavatory looks and smells like.

Leonard Clifton is writing to President Gorbachev to complain.

I said, 'I think Gorbachev has other things on his mind at the moment, such as preventing civil war and feeding his fellow citizens.'

A harmless remark, you might think, but Clifton went mad. He screamed, 'You have ruined my holiday, Mole, with your pathetic whingeing and nasty, cynical comments.'

I was totally gobsmacked. Nobody in the group came to my defence – apart from the Brightways twins, who had already informed the group at frequent intervals that they 'loved all living things'. So anything they had to say was irrelevant. They no doubt equate my life with that of a lugworm.

Thursday   August 22nd

Hotel room – Moscow

I am staying in the 'Ukraina', near the Moskva River. It looks like a hypodermic syringe from outside. Inside, it is full of bewildered guests of all nationalities. Their bewilderment stems from the hotel staff's reluctance to pass on any information.

For instance, hardly anybody knows *where* meals are being served, or even *if* meals are being served.

For breakfast this morning I had a piece of black bread, four slices of beetroot, a sprig of fresh coriander and a cup of cold, black tea.

An American woman in the queue behind me wailed to

her husband, 'Norm, I gotta have juice.'

Norm left the queue and went up to a group of loitering waiters.

I watched him mime an orange, first on the tree and then off the tree. The waiters watched him impassively, then turned their backs on him and huddled around a portable radio. Norm returned to the queue. His wife shot him a contemptuous look.

She said, 'I just gotta have some fruit in the morning. You *know* that, Norm. You know how my system seizes up.'

Norm pulled a face indicating that he remembered *exactly* what happened to his wife's system when it seized up. I thought fondly about the bunch of bananas upstairs in my room.

They were worth their weight in gold.

At nine-thirty, most of our group gathered in the foyer of the hotel ready to start our visit to Red Square. I lurked behind a pillar, dabbing T.C.P. onto the fourteen mosquito bites which disfigured my face.

The Barnstaple twins, Monica and Stella Brightways, kept us waiting for ten minutes, claiming that they had to wait for the lift to ascend to where their room was on the nineteenth floor. Eventually we set off in a bus which seemed to have an interior exhaust pipe next to my seat at the back. I coughed and choked on the diesel fumes and made a futile attempt to open the window. The coach driver was wearing a Gorbachev badge and seemed to be in a bad mood. Our coach parked on the edge of Red Square and we got out and gathered around our Intourist guide, Natasha. She held up a red and white umbrella, and we followed behind like moronic sheep. When we got to the Square, it became obvious that something was happening, a protest march or a demonstration of some kind was taking place. I lost sight of the red and white umbrella and became lost in the crowd. I heard an ominous rumbling behind me, but was unable to move.

An old lady in a headscarf shook her fist towards the noise. She screamed something in Russian. Spittle flew out of her mouth and landed on my clean sweater. Then the crowd parted and the rumbling grew nearer and the tracks of a Russian army tank clanked past an inch away from my right shoe. The tank stopped and a young man clambered aboard and began to wave a flag. It was the hammer and sickle flag I'd been used to seeing everywhere. The crowd roared its approval. What was happening? Had Moscow Dynamo won at football? No, something more important was taking place.

A young woman who wore too much blue eyeshadow said to me, 'Englishman, today you have witnessed the end of Communism.'

'I nearly got run over by a tank,' I said.

'A proud death,' she said. I reached into my pocket for a banana to boost my blood-sugar level. I started to peel it. The young woman's eyes filled with tears. I offered her a bite, but she misinterpreted my gesture and shouted something in Russian. The crowd roared and cheered. She then turned and told me she was shouting 'Bananas for all under Yeltsin!' The crowd began to chant. Then the young woman ate my banana.

'A symbolic gesture, of course,' she said.

When I returned to my room, I found a hefty young Russian woman sitting on a chair outside the door. She was wearing a low-cut brown lamé minidress.

She said, 'Ah, Mr Mole, I am Lara. I come to your room, to sleep, of course.'

I said, 'Is this part of the Intourist programme?'

Lara said, 'No. I am, of course, in love with you.'

She followed me into my room and went to the bunch of bananas on the bedside table. She looked down at them with lust in her eyes and I understood. It wasn't me she wanted: it was the bananas. I gave her two. She went away. Intercourse with her might have done me some harm. She had thighs like Californian redwoods.

Friday   August 23rd

I lay awake most of the night, scratching at my mosquito bites and regretting my hasty decision and wondering how news about my bananas had spread. The next day the streets were full of rioting Muscovites and we were confined to the hotel.

After lunch (black bread, beetroot soup, a wizened piece of meat, one cold potato), I returned to my room to find that my bananas had gone. I was outraged.

I complained to Natasha, but she only said, 'You had *ten* bananas?' She looked misty-eyed and then snapped, 'You should, of course, have put them in the hotel safe. They will be changing hands on the black market by now.'

I found Leonard Clifton in the gloomy basement bar. There had been a coup against Gorbachev and then a counter-coup by Boris Yeltsin.

'This is bad news for Soviet Communism,' he said, 'but good news for Jesus.'

England! England! England!

I long for my attic room.

Monday   September 2nd

Oxford

I am in bed, exhausted and hideously deformed. Why do mosquitoes exist? Why? Cassandra said they are 'a vital component of the food chain'. Well, I Adrian Mole, would gladly *pull* the chain on them. And, if the food chain collapses and the world starves, so be it.

I have written to Foreign Parts, threatening to report them to A.B.T.A. unless I receive *all* my money back, plus compensation for the double trauma suffered from the mosquitoes and the revolution.

Tuesday   September 3rd

Christian passed by Foreign Parts today. He said it looked deserted. There was a pile of unopened letters on the doormat inside the shop.

Thursday   September 5th

A reply from John Tydeman, Head of Drama, BBC Radio.

> Dear Adrian,
> To be perfectly honest, Adrian, my heart sank when I returned from holiday and saw that your manuscript, *Lo! The Flat Hills of My Homeland* had landed on my desk yet again. You say in your letter, 'I expect you are busy'. Yes, I damned well *am* busy, incredibly so.
>
> What exactly is a 'coffee break'? I've never had a 'coffee break' during the whole of my long career with the BBC.

I drink coffee at my desk. I do not go to a 'coffee break' lounge where I loll about on a sofa and read handwritten manuscripts, 473 pages long. My advice to you (without reading your wretched MS) is to:

1) Learn to type
2) Cut it by at least half
3) Supply a S.A.E. and postage. The BBC is suffering from a cash crisis. It certainly cannot afford to subsidise your literary outpourings.
4) Find yourself a *publisher*. I am *not* a publisher. I am the Head of Radio Drama. Though sometimes I wonder if I am Marjorie Proops.

I am sorry to have to write to you in such terms, but in my experience it is best to be frank with young writers.
          Yours, with best wishes,
               John Tydeman

Poor old Tydeman! He has obviously gone mad. 'Sometimes I wonder if I am Marjorie Proops' (!) – perhaps the Director General should be told that his Head of Radio Drama is suffering from the delusion that he is an agony aunt.

And he admitted that he hadn't even read the re-edited *Lo! What do we licence-payers pay for?*

Dear Mr Tydeman,
I would appreciate it if you could send my MS back, A.S.A.P. I do not want it circulating around the corridors of the BBC and being purloined by a disaffected freelance producer, anxious to make his or her mark on the world of broadcasting.
          Adrian Mole

P.S. Allow me to inform you, sir, that you are *not* Marjorie Proops.

Saturday   September 7th

Spent most of the day in a futile search for a reasonably priced room. As I made my weary way back home, I passed Foreign Parts. There was a note on the door:

This business is closed. All enquiries to Churchman,
Churchman, Churchman and Luther, Solicitors.

I didn't take down the telephone number. It was already in my
filofax, under 'S'. A middle-aged couple *were* taking the number
down, though. They were due to depart tomorrow on a cycling
holiday in 'Peter Mayle Country', Provence. They were facing
the awful realisation that they were not going to see the famous
table on the infamous terrace, and possibly take tea with Pierre
Mayle plus *femme*.

As the couple walked away, I heard her say to him: 'Cheer up,
Derek, there's always the caravan at Ingoldmells.' A fine woman,
indomitable in the face of disaster. Mr Mayle has been cheated
of meeting a true Brit.

Sunday   September 8th

I have decided to go with Jake Westmorland.

> *Chapter Seventeen: Jake – A Hero of Our Time*
> Jake stood on top of the tank in Red Square. What a
> good job I took Russian at school, instead of French, he
> thought. Then, quieting the multitudes by a small gesture
> of his hand, he spoke.
> 'I am Jake Westmorland,' he shouted. The revolutionary
> hordes bellowed their grateful recognition. A sea of ban-
> ners waved joyously. The sultry Russian sunlight glinted
> on the dome of St Basil's Cathedral as Jake tried to
> quieten the crowds and begin his speech. The speech
> that he hoped would prevent the disintegration of the
> Soviet Union. . . .

Monday   September 9th

I have written eleven speeches for Jake and thrown them all
in the bin. None of them was capable of changing the course
of world history.

> . . . But before Jake could make the speech that would
> almost certainly have saved the Soviet Union, a shot rang
> out and Jake fell off the tank and into the arms of Natasha,

his Russian mistress. She threw Jake over her shoulder and the silent crowd parted to let them through.

Thursday   September 12th

Cassandra has ordered me to be out of the house by noon on Saturday! The lousy, stinking undergraduates have hogged all the private rented accommodation. I had no choice but to throw myself on the mercy of Oxford Council. But the Council official I spoke to today maintained that I am 'intentionally homeless' and refused to help me. I have started collecting cardboard boxes. Either to pack my belongings in, or to sleep in – who knows?

Friday   September 13th

Christian has taken the children to see his mother in Wigan. He is a spineless coward. The hideous Cassandra is walking around the house in her absurd clothes, singing her ludicrous rapping songs. I asked her tonight if I could store my books in the attic until I've found a place of my own. She replied, 'Books?' as though she'd never heard the word before.

I said, 'Yes, *books*. You know, those things with cardboard covers stuffed with paper. People read them, for pleasure.'

Cassandra snorted contemptuously. 'Books belong in the past, together with stiletto heels and Gerry and the Pacemakers. This is the nineties, Adrian. It's the age of technology.'

She went to her word processor and pressed a button. A series of little green men wearing Viking helmets filled the screen and began to fight with little red men wearing baseball caps, who came out of a cave. Cassandra leaned eagerly towards the screen. I sensed that our conversation was over and left the room.

Query: Is the world going mad, or is it me?

Saturday   September 14th

8.30 a.m.

> *Options*
> 1) Pandora (no chance)

2) Bianca (possible)
3) Mother (last resort)
4) Bed and breakfast (expensive)
5) Hostel (fleas, violence)
6) Streets

11.30 a.m.

1) Pandora turned me down flat. She is a true *Belle Dame sans Merci*.
2) Bianca is away attending a Guns 'n' Roses convention in Wolverhampton. Left note at newsagent's.
3) My mother is out gawping at a new crop circle just outside Kettering.
4) The cheapest B&B is £15.99 a *night*!
5) There is nothing under 'Hostel' in the phone book.
6) I hit the road at high noon.

11.35 p.m. Leicester. Bert Baxter's house
So, it has come to this. I am reduced to sleeping on a Put-U-Up in a pensioner's living-room, which stinks of cats.Baxter is charging me £5 for tonight, plus £2.50 for bacon and eggs. My mother's house is locked and dark, and the key is not in its usual place under the drain cover. In normal circumstances I would have broken the small pantry window and climbed in, but my mother has had a security system installed. Delusions of grandeur, or what?

My father, supposedly penniless, is on holiday in Florida with a rich divorcee called Belinda Bellingham. I know I could go to my grandma's but I can't bear her to find out that I am unemployed and homeless. The shock could kill her. She has my G.C.S.E. certificates framed on the hall wall. My 'A' level English certificate is in a silver frame on the mantelpiece in her front room. Why give such anguish to an elderly diabetic?

Monday   September 16th

1.35 a.m. I am now trying to sleep on the sofa-bed in my mother's living room. As I write, the television in my mother's bedroom is blaring. The washing machine is on its spin cycle. The dishwasher is shrieking and somebody is taking a shower.

Subsequently, the water pipes are banging all over the house. My stepfather, Martin Muffet, has just gone upstairs with his D.I.Y. toolbox. Does nobody sleep in this house?

Tuesday   September 17th

My grandma knows all. My mother has told her everything. She is disgusted. I hope she never finds out that Bert Baxter gave me a bed for the night.

Wednesday   September 18th

G. knows about B&B at B.B.'s. She saw B.B. in C&A.

Friday   September 20th

A postcard of Clifton Suspension Bridge came this morning.

> Dear Adrian,
> I've only just got your message! Sorry I didn't see you before you left. That Cassandra is a sad woman all right!
> I've never been to Leicester. Is it nice? Hope so for your sake!
> There's a floor here for you if you fancy coming back to Oxford! I know where I can borrow a double mattress.
> Let me know soon, please!
> Love,
> B.

The exclamation marks gave me some pain. Could I share a floor with a woman who was so profligate with them? And what would the sleeping arrangements be? This 'double mattress' she mentioned. Was it for me only? If so, why a double? I presume she has an adequate bed of her own. I decided to write an ambiguous reply, keeping my options open, but committing myself to nothing. My mother, who had brought the postcard to me in bed, wanted to know *everything* about 'B'. Height, weight, build, colouring, education, class, accent, clothes, shoes. 'Is she nice?' Have I 'slept with her'? 'Why not?' The Spanish Inquisition would be nothing compared to my mother. Nothing.

Dear Bianca,

It was most kind of you to write to me and offer the use of a double mattress and your floor.

I confess to you that when I asked you for your help in solving my temporary difficulty regarding my lack of accommodation, I was in somewhat of a panic.

I am surprised that you responded as you did. Ours has not been a long acquaintanceship. For all you know, I could have severe character faults or a psychotic personality.

I would urge caution in the future. I would not like to see you taken advantage of. I am not sure about my future plans. Leicester has a certain *je ne sais quoi*: it is quite pleasant in the autumn, when the fallen leaves give the pavements a little colour.

> Yours,
> > Best wishes,
> > Adrian

Sunday   September 22nd

I was looking forward to a traditional Sunday dinner with Yorkshire pudding and gravy, etc. But my mother informed me at 1.00 p.m. that she doesn't *do* Sunday dinner any more. Instead, we were driven four miles in Muffet's car to a 'Carvery' where we paid £4.99 a head to be served with slices of cardboard and dried up vegetables by a moronic youth in a chef's hat. My sister Rosie spilt Muffet's half pint of Ruddles all over our table. I tried to come to the rescue with half a dozen beer mats – but the beer mats refused to soak up any beer. They repelled all liquid. In the end, the moronic one threw us a stinking dishcloth.

Query: What is the purpose of modern beer mats? Are they now merely symbolic, like the crucifix?

6.00 p.m. My mother has informed me that I have got to pay her board of 'a minimum of thirty-five pounds a week, or you're out on your ear'. Does blood count for nothing in 1991?

Tuesday   September 24th

My grandma has said I can move in with her, rent free, providing I cut the grass, wind the clocks and fetch the shopping. I agreed immediately.

Wednesday   September 25th

I read the first three chapters of *Lo!* aloud to Grandma tonight. She thinks it is the best thing she has ever heard. She thinks that the publishers who rejected it are barmy. And she has got nothing but contempt for Mr John Tydeman. She recently wrote to him to complain about the sex in *The Archers*. She claims that he didn't reply personally. Apparently he got a machine to do it for him.

Sunday   September 29th

Archers omnibus. Egg, bacon, fried bread, *The People*. Roast beef, roast potatoes, mashed potatoes, cabbage, carrots, peas, Yorkshire pudding, gravy. Apple crumble, custard, cup of tea, extra strong mints, *News of the World*. Tinned salmon sandwiches, mandarin oranges and jelly, sultana cake, cup of tea.

Monday   September 30th

Chapter Eighteen: Back to the Wolds
Jake settled back in the rocking chair and watched his grandmother making the corn dolly. Her apple cheeks glowed in the flames from the black leaded range. The copper kettle sang. The canary in the cage by the window trilled along with it. Jake sighed a deep, contented sigh. It was good to be back from Russia and all that unpleasantness with Natasha. Here, he could truly relax, in his grandma's cottage on the Wolds.

Tuesday   October 1st

My father brought Mrs Belinda Bellingham round to meet me at Grandma's house tonight. I was totally gobsmacked; she is a posh person! My father has started to pronounce his aitches religiously and to say 'barth' instead of 'bath'. And he has also discovered manners: every time my grandma came into the room, he leapt out of his chair.

Eventually she snapped, 'Sit *down*, George. You're up and down like a window cleaner's ladder.'

Mrs Bellingham is blonde and pretty, with those cheekbones that denote centuries of wise breeding. I thought she was very pale, considering she had just spent two weeks in the sun. Later in the evening, I found out that she lives in fear of skin cancer. Apparently she spent her holiday running from one patch of shade to another. Mrs Bellingham is the managing director of 'Bell Safe' – a burglar alarm company. My father starts work next Monday as Mrs Bellingham's sales director. They tried to persuade my grandma to allow them to install a burglar alarm at cost price, but she refused, saying, 'No, thank you. If I have to go out, I turn the volume up on Radio Four and leave my front door open.'

Mrs Bellingham and my father exchanged scandalised glances. Grandma continued, 'And I've never been burgled in sixty years, and anyroad up, if I had an alarm on the front of the house, folks'd know I've got something valuable, wouldn't they?'

There was an awkward pause, then my father said, 'Well, Belinda, I'll see you home, shall I?'

He fetched her coat and held it out while she put it on. He has obviously been having lessons in social etiquette. When they'd gone, my grandma shocked me by saying, 'Your dad's turned into a right brown-nosing bugger, hasn't he?'

Perhaps she is suffering from the early symptoms of senile dementia. I have never heard her swear before.

Sir Alan Green, the Director of Public Prosecutions, has been caught talking to a prostitute and has resigned. Under the 1985 Sexual Offences Act, a man seen approaching a woman more than once can be stopped by the police. This is news to me. I shall certainly be more careful whom I approach in the street from now on.

Friday   October 4th

Grandma and I have scoured the house from top to bottom today. Grandma has a fixation about germs. She is convinced that they are lying in wait for her, ready to pounce and bring her down. I blame the television advertisement for a lavatory cleaner which depicts 'germs' the size of gremlins, who lurk about in the 'S' bend, chuckling malevolently. Although I've seen this advertisement hundreds of times, I simply can't remember what the product is called.

Query: Is television advertising effective?

Later, Grandma sat down and watched the Labour Party singing 'We Are the Champions' as the finale to their conference in Brighton. Not many of the shadow cabinet knew the words. I hope Freddie Mercury wasn't watching – it would have stuck in his teeth, not to mention his craw.

Sunday   October 6th

Turning the pages of my *Observer* today, I saw Barry Kent's ugly face staring out at me. Apparently he is a new member of a place called the Groucho Club. I read the accompanying article avidly. It is exactly the sort of place I would like to be a member of. Should I ever reach that goal, I shall tell the manager (Liam) the truth about Kent's past and have him blackballed.

Elizabeth Taylor has married a bricklayer with a bad perm. He is called Larry Fortensky. Michael Jackson's ape, Bubbles, was the best man.

Chapter Nineteen: Time to Move On

Jake slipped out of the cottage as the village church struck midnight. He ran stealthily down the lane and towards the minicab which was waiting, as instructed, by the post office. As he threw his rucksack into the back of the car and climbed in after it, he sighed with relief. He never again wanted to see the apple cheeks of his grandmother and he vowed to burn the next corn dolly he came across.

'Put your foot down!' Jake barked to the minicab driver. 'Take me to the nearest urban conurbation.'

The minicab driver's brow was furrowed. 'What's an urban conurbation when it's at 'ome?' he said.

Jake snapped, 'Okay, dolt! You want specifics, take me to the Groucho Club.'

At the mention of the magic words, the cab driver's shoulders straightened. The dandruff stayed on his scalp. He had waited years to hear the words, 'Take me to the Groucho Club'. He looked at Jake with a new respect and he did as he was told. He put his foot down on the clutch and the minicab sped away from the Wolds and towards the great metropolis where, in the Groucho, the Great were no doubt quaffing the house wine and exchanging witticisms. Jake hoped Belinda would be there, at the bar, showing her legs and laughing hysterically at one of Jeffrey Bernard's jokes.

Monday October 7th

Barry Kent is making a film for BBC2 about his 'roots'. The television cameras were in the Co-op, blocking the aisles. I couldn't get to the cat food, so I complained to the manager (who, incidentally, didn't look a day older than seventeen). He replied, 'Barry Kent's comin' here in person this afternoon.' It was as though he were talking about royalty.

I said, 'I don't give a toss. I want three tins of Whiskas, *now*!' The boy manager went off and, in crawling tones, asked the cameraman to pass him three tins of cat food. With what I thought was ill grace, the cameraman obliged and, after paying the starstruck child, I left the shop.

Tuesday   October 8th

My mother has been persuaded to give a talk to camera about 'the Barry Kent she once knew'. I urged her to tell the truth, about the bullying, lying, scruffy, thick youth we knew and despised.

But my mother said, 'I always found Barry to be a sensitive child.' The director made her stand by her overflowing wheelie bin in the side yard.

My mother said, 'Shouldn't I be made-up, by a proper make-up artist?' Nick, the director, said, 'No, Mrs Mole, we're going for actuality.' My mother touched the cold sore on her lip and said, 'I'd counted on a bit of camouflage to hide this.' A strong light was turned on her, which showed every line, wrinkle and bag on my mother's face.

Then the director shouted, 'Go!' and my mother went. To pieces. After seventeen attempts, BBC2 gave up, packed their gear and went off. My mother ran upstairs and threw herself on the bed. There is nothing so pitiful as a failed interviewee.

Saturday   October 12th

Kent is still poncing around the neighbourhood. I saw him being filmed walking up our street. He was wearing a floor-length overcoat, cowboy boots and dark glasses. I ducked out of sight. I have no wish to be publicly identified as the dork in *Dork's Diary*.

I took the dog for a walk to the field where Pandora used to ride Blossom, her pony. It tired very quickly. I had to carry it back.

I saw Mrs Kent, Barry's mother, on the way home. She was walking her pit bull terrier. I asked her if she had registered the beast yet (as required by law).

She said, 'Butcher wouldn't hurt a fly.'

I said, 'It's not flies I'm worried about. It's the tender flesh of small children.'

She changed the subject and told me that Barry had bought her the council house she now lives in. This made me laugh quite a lot. The Kents' house is a byword for squalor in our neighbourhood. They chop the internal doors up for firewood every winter.

Sunday October 13th

Finished Chapter Nineteen tonight.

> Jake was sick of being interviewed. He ordered the jour-
> nalists to leave the Groucho Club and leave him alone. He
> turned to Lenny Henry and said, 'Let's have a drink, Len.'
> Lenny smiled his thanks and Jake snapped his fingers. A
> waiter came running immediately and bent deferentially
> towards Jake. 'A bottle of champagne – a big one – and
> make that three glasses,' for Jake had just seen one of his
> best friends, Richard Ingrams, of *News Quiz* fame, come
> through the hallowed swing doors. 'Hey, Rich, over here!'
> shouted Jake. There was a sound of scuffling coming from
> the reception area. Jake turned his head round to see Liam,
> the manager, throwing Kent Barry, the failed writer, out of
> the club and into the gutter.

Monday October 14th

> Dear Bianca,
>   After further reflection, can I take you up on your
> offer? It would be most convenient for me to spend a
> few days sleeping on your floor in Oxford. Quite honestly,
> I cannot tolerate another moment living with my family. It
> isn't just the noise level and the constant bickering; it's the
> small things – the encrusted neck of the H.P. Sauce bottle;
> the slimy soap dish; the dog hairs in the butter. You can
> telephone me on the above number, any time, night or day.
> Nobody sleeps in this house.
>   All my very best wishes,
>   Adrian Mole

Tuesday October 15th

My sister Rosie told me that she hated me this morning. Her outburst came after I suggested that she comb her hair before going
to school. My mother got out of bed and came downstairs. She lit
her second cigarette of the day (she smokes the first in bed) and

immediately took Rosie's side. She said, 'Leave the kid alone.'

I said, 'Somebody has to maintain standards in this house.'

My mother said, 'You can talk. That beard looks like a ferret's nest. I don't know how you can bear to have it so near to your mouth. A public health inspector would close it down.'

During the ensuing row, nasty things were said on both sides, which I now regret. I accused her of being a neglectful mother, with loose morals. She counter-attacked by describing me as 'a fungus-faced dork'. She said she had secretly read my *Lo!* manuscript and thought it was 'crap from start to finish'. She said 'in the unlikely event of it being published, I hope you will use a pseudonym, because, to be honest, Adrian, I couldn't stand the public shame.'

I put my head on the kitchen table and wept.

My mother then put her arm around me and said, 'There, there, Adrian. Don't cry. I didn't mean it, I think *Lo! The Flat Hills of My Homeland* is a very interesting first attempt.'

But it was no good. I wept until dehydration set in.

10.00 p.m. Why hasn't Bianca phoned? I used a first class stamp.

Thursday   October 17th

Drew more money out of the Market Harborough Building Society. My dream of being an owner-occupier has receded even further into the realms of fantasy.

I have received a postcard of the Forth Bridge, with no address but posted in London.

> Dear Adrian,
> I'm going to London to try for a proper job. I've got an interview with British Rail. In a rush. Please reply c/o my friend Lucy:
>
>> Lucy Clay
>> Flat 10
>> Dexter House
>> Coghill Street
>> Oxford
>
> She has promised to pass on any messages. I hope you

are well and happy. I miss you!
 Love,
  B.
P.S. How about a London floor when I find one?

Friday October 18th

Chapter Twenty: The Reckoning
Jake pushed the earth wire out of the lawnmower plug, then screwed the plug together again. He could hear his mother on the telephone to her new lover (a schoolboy called Craig).

He waited for her to finish cooing her endearments down the phone and re-emerge on the terrace. 'I've cut half the lawn, mother,' he shouted, 'but I've got to go to the barber's now.'

His mother frowned and dropped ash all down her cashmere dress. 'But Jake, darling,' she remonstrated. 'You know I hate to see a job half done.' She went towards the lawnmower.

Jake chuckled inwardly. He had banked on this trait of his mother's. As he passed through the french windows, he heard the hover-mower whir into life, to be followed immediately by the high-pitched scream.

Jake immediately felt guilty, then comforted himself by thinking that he had advised his mother time after time to install a circuit breaker; advice she had foolishly chosen to ignore.

Sunday October 20th

It was my father's access day today. He came to take Rosie out to McDonald's as usual. While she looked for her shoes, my father and I talked man to man about my mother. We agreed that she was an impossible person to live with. We had a good laugh about Martin Muffet, who was in the back garden building a lean-to conservatory with the assistance of his Black and Decker work bench. We agreed that, since marrying my mother, Muffet has aged ten years.

I congratulated my father on capturing Mrs Belinda Bellingham, and confessed that I didn't have much luck with women.

My father said, 'Tell them what they want to hear, son, and buy them a bunch of flowers once a fortnight. That's all there is to it.'

I asked him if he intended to marry Mrs Bellingham, but before he could answer, my mother staggered into the room carrying a large cardboard box which contained the swag she'd bought from a car boot sale. She'd bought a painting of Christ on the cross; an ashtray with two scottie dogs painted on it; an aluminium toast rack; twenty-seven bent candles; a chenille tablecloth; a Tom Jones LP; six cooking apples; and a steering wheel. As she excitedly unpacked the junk onto the kitchen table, I saw my father looking at her with what I can only describe as lovelight in his eyes.

Monday   October 21st

Bianca rang, but I was out cutting Bert Baxter's disgusting toe-nails. My mother wrote down a telephone number where I could contact Bianca, but then lost it almost immediately. We searched the house, but failed to find the scrap of paper. I expect the dog ate it. It has recently taken to scoffing whole pages of the *Leicester Mercury*, a sign of its increasing neurosis or a vitamin deficiency – who knows? Nobody can afford to take it to the vet to find out.

Tuesday   October 22nd

I sent a postcard of Leicester Bus Station to Bianca c/o Lucy Clay:

> Dear Bianca,
> Thank you for your postcard of the Forth Bridge.
>   I was most surprised to hear that you were leaving Oxford and going to the 'Smoke', as the cockneys say.
>   I wish you luck in your search for a 'proper' job. Keep me posted. I have had no luck yet, but I keep trying.
>   It is very difficult living here with my family. There is a total clash of lifestyles. I strive to be tolerant of the noise and disorder, but it is hard, very hard.
>   Yours,
>   With very best wishes,
>   Adrian

Mrs Bellingham has offered me a job selling security devices.

It is evening work. I have to call on nervous householders after dark and put the fear of God into them until they sign up for a burglar alarm or security lights. I said I would think about it.

Mrs Bellingham said in her careful voice, 'There are three million unemployed. Why do you need to think about it?'

I said I hoped that beggars could still be choosers.

She is offering me £3.14 an hour. No commission, no insurance stamp, no contract of employment – cash in hand. I asked her if she objected to my belonging to a union. Her face went whiter than ever and she said, 'Yes, I'm afraid I do. Mrs Thatcher's greatest achievement was to tame the unions.' My father is a Thatcherite's lackey!

Thursday October 24th

I despise myself. I have only been working for two nights, but I have already sold a whole house security system, six car alarms, four peepholes and half a dozen bike locks. My method is simple. I get into the house and show the householders the portfolio that Mrs Bellingham has assembled. It consists of lurid stories cut out of the tabloid newspapers and police press releases. After leafing through this alarming document, it would take great insouciance for the householder to deny that more security in the home is a desirable thing.

Mrs Bellingham has instructed me to ask the question, 'Don't you think your family deserves more protection from the dark forces of evil that are at large in our community?'

So far only one person has said, 'No,' and he was the defeated-looking father of six teenage boys.

Monday October 28th

Shaved beard off. Mrs Bellingham said it made me look untrustworthy. I am completely in her power. If she ordered me to go to work wearing a Batman outfit, I would have to obey her. I have no legal rights of employment.

Thursday October 31st

At last! The economic recovery is on its way! The Confederation of British Industry has reported that they expect outputs and exports to increase in the years ahead. According to the C.B.I., manufacturers are expecting huge new orders. I broke this good news to my mother. She said, 'Yes, and the dog is getting married on Saturday and I'm its Matron of Honour.' Then she and Martin Muffet went off into one of their mad laughing fits.

Ken Barlow of *Coronation Street* fame has been on trial for being boring. He was found 'Not Guilty' and awarded £50,000.

My mother has got a job as a security guard in the new shopping centre that has just opened in Leicester city centre. She looks like a New York City policewoman in her uniform. She told the security firm, 'Group Five', that she was *thirty-five years old*! She is now living in fear that her true age, forty-seven, will be revealed. Is everybody partially sighted at Group Five? Did her interview take place in a candlelit office? I asked her these questions.

She said, 'I bunged on rather a lot of Max Factor's pan-stick and sat with my back to the window.'

Friday   November 1st

In view of my continuing success in flogging her security paraphernalia, Mrs Bellingham has raised my hourly rate from £3.14 to the heady sum of £3.25! Gee whiz! Fire a cannon! Release the balloons! Open the Bollinger! Issue a press release! Inform the Red Arrows!

Saturday   November 2nd

Jake used his Swiss Army knife to dismantle the burglar alarm and in a matter of moments he had circumnavigated the padlocks, bolts and chains on the front door and was standing in the front hall of Bellingham Towers.

Upstairs, sleeping after an hour of arduous lovemaking, were the owners of the historic country house, Sir George and Lady Belinda, and their daughter, the Honourable Rosemary. Jake chuckled as he stuffed silver and *objets d'art* into a black plastic bag. He felt no guilt. He was robbing the filthy rich to feed the filthy poor. He was the Robin Hood of Leicestershire.

My mother claims that I look exactly like John Major, especially when I am wearing my reading glasses. This is total rubbish: unlike Mr Major, I have got lips. They may be on the thin side, but they are distinctly there. If I were Major, I'd have a lip transplant. Mick Jagger could be the donor.

Tuesday   November 5th

Robert Maxwell, the mogul, has fallen overboard from his yacht, the *Lady Ghislaine*.

Went to Age Concern Community Bonfire Party. Pushed Bert Baxter there in his wheelchair. Baxter was asked to leave after half an hour because he was seen (and certainly heard) to throw an Indian firecracker into the bonfire. The organiser, Mrs Plumbstead, said apologetically, 'Safety has to be paramount.'

Baxter said scornfully, 'There were no such thing as *safety* when I were a lad.'

I pushed him home in silence. I was furious. Because of him, I missed the baked potatoes, sausages and soup. I had to wait for an hour for the district nurse to come and put him to bed.

Thursday   November 7th

Kevin Maxwell has denied that his deceased father's businesses have financial problems.

Query: Would our banks lend £2.5 billion to a man with money problems?

Answer: Of course not! Our banks are respected financial institutions.

Sunday   November 10th

To Grandma's for the Remembrance Day poppy-laying ceremony. I am proud of my dead grandfather, Albert Mole. He fought valiantly in the First World War so that I would not have to live under the tyranny of a foreign oppressor.

I cannot let the above sentence lie. The truth is that my poor, dead grandfather fought in the Great War because he was ordered to. He always did what he was told. I take after him in that respect.

Monday   November 11th

A gang of Leicester yobs shouted out, 'Hey, John Major, how's Norma?' tonight, as I came out of the cinema. I looked around, thinking that perhaps the Prime Minister was visiting the Leicester Chamber of Commerce, or something, but there was no sign of him. I then realised, to my horror, that they were addressing their yobbish remarks to me.

Wednesday   November 13th

A letter from Bianca.

> Dear Adrian,
> Thank you for your letter, which Lucy forwarded to me. As you can see from my address, I am living in London. I am renting a small room in Soho at the moment, but it is costing £110 per week, so I won't be here long!
> I've got a job as a waitress in a restaurant called 'Savages'. The owner is a bit strange, but the staff are very nice. It would be lovely to see you when you're next in London. My day off is Monday. How is the novel going? Have you finished your revisions? I can't wait to read it in full!
> Love,
> Bianca (Dartington)

Thursday   November 14th

> Dear Bianca,
> Many thanks for your letter of the 11th. I must confess that I was rather surprised to hear from you. I am hardly ever in London, but I may drop in and see you on my next visit. Isn't Soho a dangerous place in which to live? Please take care as you walk the streets. Personally, I am ossifying in this provincial hell.

Lo! is going very well. I have called my hero Jake Westmorland. What do you think?

Please write back.

Yours as ever,
Adrian

Friday   November 15th

The New York Stock Exchange collapsed today. I hope this won't affect the interest rates of the Market Harborough Building Society.

Saturday   November 16th

No reply from B.

Sunday   November 17th

Why isn't there a Sunday delivery in this country? I expect it is because of objections from the established Church. Do the clergy imagine that God gives a toss if humans receive letters or not on a Sunday?

Monday   November 18th

By second post. A postcard of Holborn Viaduct.

Dear Adrian,
No. Soho is not dangerous. I *love* Jake Westmorland. When are you coming to London?
Lots of love,
Bianca

Tuesday   November 19th

I sent Bianca a postcard of the Clock Tower, Leicester.

Dear Bianca,
As it happens, I shall be in London next Monday. Would

you like to have lunch? Please write or ring to confirm.
Very warm wishes,
Adrian

P.S. I have shaved my beard off. It was the television
pictures of Terry Waite that decided me.

Wednesday November 20th

Grandma's Christmas card arrived. The shops are full of
Santa Clauses ringing bells and getting in the way of legitimate
shoppers. My mother said that whilst on duty she saw an old lady
shoplifting a Cadbury's Selection Box. I asked her what action
she'd taken. She said, 'I turned and walked the other way.'

There is a rush on for burglar alarms. Everybody wants
them fitted before Christmas when they fill their homes with
consumer durables and Nintendo games.

Saturday November 23rd

A postcard from Bianca, of the original Crystal Palace.

Dear Adrian,
I have got to work on Monday. The office party season
has started, but come down anyway. I will get off early.
I look forward to seeing you. Come to 'Savages', Dean
Street, at 2.30 p.m.
Love,
Bianca

Sunday November 24th

Freddie Mercury has died of Aids. There was no time for me
to mourn, but I put 'Bohemian Rhapsody', which is one of my
favourite records, on the record player.

I laid my wardrobe on my bed (or rather, the *contents* of
my wardrobe) and tried to decide what to wear for my trip
to London. I do not wish to be marked out as a provincial
day-tripper by sneering metropolitans. Decided on the black
shirt, black trousers and Oxfam tweed jacket. My grey slip-on
shoes will have to do. Set my alarm for 8.30 a.m. I catch the
12.30 p.m. train.

Monday   November 25th

Soho

I am in love with Bianca Dartington. Hopelessly, helplessly, mindlessly, gloriously, magnificently.

Tuesday   November 26th

I am still here, in Soho, in Bianca's room above Brenda's Patisserie in Old Compton Street. I have hardly seen daylight since 3.30 p.m. on Monday.

Wednesday   November 27th

Poem to Bianca Dartington:

> Gentle face,
> Night black hair,
> Natural grace,
> Love I swear.
> Marry me, be my wife,
> Make me happy, share my life.

Thursday   November 28th

Phoned my mother and asked her to send my books to Old Compton Street. Informed her that I am now living in London, with Bianca. She asked for the address, but I wasn't falling for that. I hung up.

Friday   November 29th

God, I love her! I love her! I love her! Every minute she is away, working at 'Savages', is torture for me.

Query: Why didn't I *know* that the human body is capable of such exquisite pleasure?

Answer: Because, Mole, you had not made love to Bianca Dartington – somebody who loves you body and soul – before.

Saturday November 30th

What did I ever see in Pandora Braithwaite? She is an opinionated, arrogant ball-breaker. An all-round nasty piece of work. Compared to Bianca, she is nothing, nothing. And as for Leonora De Witt, I can hardly remember her face.

I never want to leave this room. I want to live the whole of my life within these four walls (with occasional trips to the bathroom, which we have to share with a fire-eater called Norman).

The walls are painted lavender blue and Bianca has stuck stars and moons on the ceiling which glow in the dark. There is a poster of Sydney Harbour Bridge on the wall between the windows. There is a double bed with an Indian bedspread covered in cushions; a chest of drawers that Bianca has painted white; an old armchair covered in a large tablecloth. A wonky table, half painted in gold, and two pine chairs. Instead of a bedhead, we have got a blown-up photograph on the wall of Isambard Kingdom Brunel, Bianca's hero.

Every morning when I wake up, I can't believe that the slim girl with the long legs who is lying next to me is mine! I always get out of bed first and put the kettle on the Baby Belling cooker. I then put two slices of toast under the grill and serve my love with her breakfast in bed. I won't allow her to get out of bed until the gas fire has warmed the room. She catches cold easily.

I want to please her more than I want to please myself.

This morning, 'Stand By Me', sung by Ben E. King, was playing on Capital Radio.

I said, 'I love this song. My father used to play it.'

Bianca said, 'So do I.'

We danced to it, me in my boxer shorts and Bianca in her pink knickers with the flowers on.

'Stand By Me' is now our song.

Sunday December 1st

Went to the National Gallery today. We walked around the Sainsbury Wing like Siamese twins, fused together. We cannot bear to be apart for even a moment. The renaissance pictures glowed like jewels and inflamed our passion. Our mutual genitalia are a bit sore and bruised, but it didn't stop us making love as soon as we got back to the room. Norman next door banged on the wall and nearly put us off, but we managed to ignore him.

Monday   December 2nd

I was putting my socks and shoes on this morning, when I noticed a strange expression on Bianca's face.

I said, 'What is it, darling?'

After a lot of cajoling, Bianca confessed that she adored everything about me except my grey slip-on shoes and white towelling socks. As a mark of my love for her, I opened the window and hurled my only pair of socks and shoes into Old Compton Street. I was unable to go out all day as a consequence. I was a barefoot prisoner of love.

Late that afternoon, Bianca bought me three pairs of socks from Sock Shop, and one pair of dark brogues from Bally. They all fitted perfectly. The shoes are *serious*. I felt like a grown-up in them as I walked around the room. I then walked to the Nat West Bank in Wardour Street and removed £100 from the Rapid Cash machine. This is the most I have ever withdrawn in one go. I paid Bianca for the shoes (£59.99), which is also the most I have ever paid for a pair of shoes. Incidentally, it is now late evening and the grey slip-ons are still in the gutter. I *did* see a tramp try them on, but he scowled and took them off immediately, though they looked a good fit.

Wednesday   December 4th

I telephoned my mother today and asked her why she hadn't sent my books on as I had asked.

She screamed, 'Mainly because you refused to give me your address, you stupid sod.' She then went on to say that she had asked our postman, Courtney Elliot, for an estimate of the cost of sending the books by Parcel Post. Apparently, he 'guestimated' (her word, not mine) that it would cost about a hundred quid! She said that my father is driving to London on Friday to attend a conference on Home Security. She said she would ask him to drop the books, and the rest of my worldly goods, off. I agreed reluctantly and gave her the address.

When Bianca had gone to work, I walked to Oxford Street and bought a dustpan and brush, a packet of yellow dusters, Mr Sheen, a floor cloth, some liquid Flash, a bottle of Windolene and a pair of white satin knickers from Knickerbox.

Bianca was thrilled when she returned at 3.00 p.m. to find our room cleaned and sparkling. Almost as thrilled as I was at 1.00 a.m. when she put the satin knickers on.

Friday   December 6th

My father was in a foul temper when he got here tonight. The conference was in Watford, so he had to go considerably out of his way (backwards) in order to deliver my stuff. When he eventually found Old Compton Street, it was 9.30 p.m.

He parked outside on double yellow lines, with his hazard lights flashing. Together, we lugged the boxes of books and plastic bags of clothes four floors up to the room. When we'd finished, my father collapsed on the bed. His bald patch was glistening with sweat. I was glad that Bianca was at work. When he'd recovered, I went down to see him off. Mrs Bellingham had ordered him to be home at a reasonable time. He is obviously afraid of her. As we walked to the car, my father stopped, pointed to the gutter and shouted, 'What the bleeding hell is that?'

His Montego had been wheel-clamped. I thought he was going to break down and cry in the street, but instead he went berserk and kicked at the yellow clamp and shouted obscenities. It was highly amusing to the posing idiots who were drinking cappuccino in the cold wind on the opposite pavement.

I offered to go with him to the outer reaches of London, to start the long, bureaucratic process of declamping the car, but my father snarled, 'Oh, bugger off back upstairs to your cowing love nest.' He hailed a black cab and jumped in. As it turned into Wardour Street, I could tell that it wouldn't be long before my father was whining to the cab driver about his bad luck, his ungrateful son, his fearsome mistress and his feckless ex-wife.

Saturday   December 7th

Spent a pleasant day cataloguing and then arranging my

books on the bookshelves I constructed from three planks and nine old bricks I found in a skip in Greek Street. Cost? Nil. In the same skip, I found *Moral Thinking* by John Wilson. It was printed in 1970, before sex came into *The Archers*, however, so I suppose the morality may be out of date.

Bianca came home at lunchtime and asked if I wanted a job as a part-time washer-up in 'Savages'. It is cash in hand, off the books. I said, 'Yes.'

We went to see the Thames Barrier and talked about our future. We pledged that we would not let riches and fame divide us.

I start washing up on Monday.

Monday   December 9th

Peter Savage, the owner of 'Savages', is certainly aptly named. I have never known a man with such a bad temper. He is rude to everybody, staff and customers. The customers think he is amusingly eccentric. The staff hate him and spend their meal breaks fantasising about killing him. He is a tall, fat man with a face like a beef tomato. He dresses like Bertie Wooster and talks like Bob Hoskins of *Roger Rabbit* fame. He wears a C.N.D. tiepin on his Garrick Club tie.

Culturally, he is all over the place.

Tuesday   December 10th

Savage was drunk at 10 a.m. At 12 noon he vomited into the yukka plant in the corner of the restaurant. At 1 p.m. his wife came, abused him verbally and then carried him out to her car, helped by Luigi, the head waiter.

I am reading *The Complete Plain Words* by Sir Ernest Gowers. I am on page 143: *Clichés*. Far be it from me to say so, but I'm sure my writing style will improve by leaps and bounds.

Bianca startled me this evening by suddenly shouting, 'Please, Adrian, can't you stop that perpetual sniffing. Use a handkerchief!'

Wednesday   December 11th

I toil over greasy pots and pans for £3.90 an hour, and the customers fork out £17 for a monkfish and £18 for a bottle of wine! Savage is obviously not as stupid as he looks.

Fogle, Fogle, Brimmington and Hayes, the advertising firm, held their Christmas party in 'Savages' at lunchtime. The restaurant was closed to ordinary customers. Bianca said that the managing director, Piers Fogle, told her that they were in a celebratory mood because they had just won a contract worth £500,000 on the strength of a slogan for an advertising campaign for condoms.

'What the well-dressed man is wearing,' is to appear on billboards all over the country.

Their bill came to over £700. They gave Bianca and the other waitresses £5 each. I, the serf in the kitchen, got nothing, of course. Luigi put two fingers up to Fogle's back as he staggered out of the restaurant.

Saturday   December 14th

We haven't made love for over twenty-four hours. Bianca has got cystitis.

Sunday   December 15th

Bought *The Joy of Sex* in the Charing Cross Road. Cystitis is called 'The Honeymooners' Illness'. It can be caused by vigorous, frequent sex. Poor Bianca is in the toilet every ten minutes. Why is there *always* a price to pay for pleasure?

Monday   December 16th

Savage was in court this morning, charged with assaulting a customer last April. He was fined £500 and ordered to pay costs and damages totalling my wages for five years. He came back to the restaurant with Mrs Savage and his lawyer to celebrate the fact that he hadn't been sent to prison, but after the champagne had been drunk and the tagliatelle consumed, Savage spotted a group of Channel Four executives on table eight and began to abuse them because they didn't show enough tobogganing on their sports programmes.

According to Bianca, Mrs Savage said, 'Darling, do be quiet, you're starting to get a little tedious.'

Savage shouted, 'Shut your mouth, you fat cow!'

She shouted, 'I'm a size *ten*, you callous bastard!'

The lawyer tried to conciliate, but Savage tipped the table up and Luigi ended up throwing his boss out of his own restaurant.

Personally, I would be happy to see Savage chained up in prison, on bread and water, with rats gnawing at his feet – and I'm a supporter of prison reform.

Tuesday   December 17th

Experimented with making very gentle love. I was the passive partner.

Later, we had our first argument. Where are we spending Christmas Day and Boxing Day? In our room? At her parents'? At my parents'? Or with Luigi, who has invited us to his house in Harrow? We didn't shout at each other, but there was (and still is) a distinct lack of seasonal goodwill. Bianca turned her back on me in bed tonight.

Thursday   December 19th

We woke up tangled together, as usual. Christmas wasn't mentioned, but love, passion and marriage were. We are going to spend Christmas with her parents in Richmond. Her father is going to pick us up on Christmas Eve. It will save me having to buy presents for my family.

Saturday   December 21st

Tonight, Savage promenaded around the restaurant with a miniature Christmas tree on his head, complete with twinkling lights. He kissed all the women and blew cigar smoke at all the men. Luigi led him into the kitchen and propped him up against the sink. Savage then proceeded to tell me that his mother had never loved him and that his father had run away with an alcoholic nurse when he was eight. (When Savage *junior* was eight.) He broke down and wept, but I was too busy to comfort him. The cook was screaming for side plates.

Sunday   December 22nd

Bianca stayed in bed today, tired out, poor kid, which gave me a chance to work on chapter twenty-one of *Lo! The Flat Hills of My Homeland*.

> Jake ran his fingers down the length of her back. Her skin felt like the finest silk, even to his fingers, roughened by years of immersion in washing-up water. She sighed and squirmed into the flannelette sheet. 'Don't stop,' she said, her voice cracking like a whip. 'Don't ever stop, Jake . . .'

Tuesday   December 24th

CHRISTMAS EVE

I braved the maddening crowds today and went out to buy Bianca's Christmas present. After tramping the streets for two hours, I ended up in Knickerbox and bought her a purple suspender belt, scarlet knickers, and a black lace bra. When the saleswoman asked me about size, I confessed I didn't know. I said, 'She's not Rubenesque, but she's not Naomi Campbell.'

The woman rolled her eyes and said, 'Okay, she's medium, yeah?'

I said, 'She looks a bit like Paula Yates, but with black hair.'

The woman sighed and said, 'Paula Yates breastfeeding or not breastfeeding?'

I said, 'Not breastfeeding,' and she snatched some stuff off the racks and gift-wrapped it for me.

I agonised in Burger King over whether or not to buy her parents presents. At four-thirty, I decided that, yes, I would ingratiate myself with them and bought her mother some peach-based pot-pourri. I phoned Bianca at 'Savages' and asked what I should get for her father. She said her father was fond of poetry, so I went and bought him a book of poems by John Hegley, called *Can I Come Down Now Dad?* which has a picture of Jesus on the cross on its cover. I also managed to track down a copy of *The Railway Heritage of Britain* by Gordon Biddle and O. S. Nock for Bianca.

Thursday December 26th

BOXING DAY

Richmond

Bianca's mother is allergic to peaches; and her father, the Reverend Dartington, thought that the John Hegley book was in extremely bad taste. Also, I hate Bianca's brother and sister. How my sweet, darling Bianca could have come from such a vile family is a mystery to me. We slept in separate beds in separate rooms. We had to go to a wooden hut of a church on Christmas Day and listen to her father rant on about the commercialisation of Christmas. Bianca and I were the only people to buy presents. Everyone else had given money to the Sudanese Drought Fund. Bianca bought me a Swatch watch and the *Chronicle of the Twentieth Century*, which will be an invaluable work of reference to me. I was very pleased. She was pleased with the Biddle and Nock.

Her brother, Derek, and her sister, Mary, obviously disapprove of our love affair. They are both unmarried and still live at home. Derek is thirty-five and Mary is twenty-seven. Mrs Dartington was forty-eight when Bianca was born.

There was no turkey, no drink and no celebration. It made me long for my own family's vulgarity.

This afternoon, we had to go for a walk alongside the river. Little kids were out in force, wobbling on new bikes and pushing prams with new-looking dolls inside. Derek has now taken a shine to me. He thought I was a fellow trainspotter; I quickly put him right. Bianca and I managed a quick embrace in the kitchen tonight before being interrupted by Mary, who came in looking for her constipation chocolate.

Mrs Dartington had a convenient 'turn' just before dinner and took to her bed. Bianca and I cooked the meal. We had salad, corned beef and baked potatoes. I cannot wait to get back to our room. I need Bianca. I need onions. I need garlic. I need Soho. I need Savage. I need air. I need freedom from the Dartingtons.

There are four beige car coats hanging up in the downstairs cloakroom.

Friday   December 27th

The Reverend Dartington drove us back to Soho in martyred silence. Every time he stopped at a red light or pedestrian crossing, he drummed his fingers on the steering wheel impatiently.

Two days with her family have had a deleterious effect on Bianca: she seems to have shrunk physically and regressed mentally. As soon as she got back into the room she burst into tears and shouted, 'Why didn't they *tell* me they were giving their Christmas presents to the Sudanese?'

I said, 'Because they wanted to claim the moral high ground and make you feel foolish. It's obviously a punishment because you are living in sin, in Soho, with a lowly washer-upper.'

An hour later, Bianca had sprung back in size and mental capacity. We made love for one hour, ten minutes. Our longest yet. It is quite useful having a stopwatch facility on my new Swatch.

Sunday   December 29th

We went to Camden Lock today to buy Bianca a pair of boots. The whole area was thronging with young people who were both buying and selling. I said to Bianca, 'Isn't it nice to see the young out and about and enjoying themselves?'

She looked at me in a funny way and said, 'But *you* are young. You're only twenty-four, though sometimes I find it hard to believe.'

She was right, of course. I am young, officially, but I have never felt young. My mother said I was thirty-five on the day I fought my way out of her womb.

The cystitis is back. Bianca has reluctantly put the satin knickers back in her underwear drawer and gone back to the cotton gussets.

I am reading a play, *A Streetcar Named Desire* by Tennessee Williams. Poor Blanche Dubois!

Wednesday   January 1st 1992

'Savages' was closed last night, so we went to Trafalgar Square at 11.30 p.m. to see the New Year in. The crowd was like a drunken field of corn rippling and swaying in a storm. For over two hours I lost myself and went with the flow. It was frightening, but also exhilarating to find myself in a line doing the conga up St Martin's Lane. Unfortunately, the person in front of me had extremely fat buttocks. It was not an attractive sight.

When Big Ben struck twelve, I found myself kissing and being kissed by strangers, including foreigners. I tried to get to Bianca, but she was surrounded by a party of extrovert Australian persons who were all over seven foot tall. But finally, at 12.03 a.m. on the 1st of January, we kissed and pledged our troth. I can't believe I've got such a wonderful woman. Why does she love me? I live in fear that one day she will wake up and ask herself the same question.

We went to Tower Bridge today. It left me cold, but Bianca was enraptured by the structural design of the thing. I practically had to drag her away.

Thursday   January 2nd

Got up at 3.30 a.m. and joined the queue outside Next in Oxford Street. The sale started at 9.00 a.m. I got into conversation with a man who had his eye on a double-breasted navy suit, marked down from £225 to £90. He is getting married to a parachute packer, called Melanie, next Saturday.

In my new black leather jacket, white tee shirt and blue jeans, I look like every other young man in London, New York and Tokyo. Or Leicester, come to think of it. For Leicester is at the very epicentre of the Next empire.

Bianca wanted to visit Battersea Power Station today and

asked me to go with her, but I pointed out to her that *Lo!* was about to develop in a revolutionary direction and that I needed to work on Chapter Twenty-two.

She left the flat without saying a word, but her back looked very angry.

> Jake pulled the collar of his Next black leather jacket
> up against the cruel wind that blew across the Thames.
> He stared down into the ebbing water. It was time he did
> something with his life other than help with famine relief
> in Sudan. He knew what it was. It was something he had
> fought against – God knows how he had fought! But the
> compulsion was overwhelming now. He had to do it. He
> had to write a novel. . . .

Wednesday   January 8th

President Bush vomited into the lap of the Japanese Ambassador at an official banquet in Tokyo tonight. We watched it on the portable television in the kitchen at 'Savages'. Mrs Bush shoved her husband under the table, then left the room. She didn't look too pleased. The television news showed the whole incident in slow motion. It was sickening. The Japanese people looked horrified. They are sticklers for protocol.

Savage has fired little Carlos for smoking a joint in the yard at the back of the restaurant. Savage then drank half a bottle of brandy, three bottles of Sol, stole various drinks from customers' tables and ended up fighting with the palm tree at the bar after accusing it of having an affair with his wife. Alcohol is certainly a dangerous drug in the wrong hands.

Wednesday   January 15th

> Jake sat in front of his state of the art Amstrad and
> pressed the glittery knobs. The title of his novel appeared
> on the screen.
>
> SPARG FROM KRONK
> *Chapter One: Sparg Returns*
> Sparg stood on the hilltop and looked down on Kronk,
> the settlement of his birth. He grunted to his woman,

Barf, and she grunted back wordlessly, for the words had not yet been found.

They ran down the hill. Sparg's mother, Krun, watched her son and his woman come towards the fire. She grunted to Sparg's father, Lunt, and he came to the door of the hut. His eyes narrowed. He hated Sparg.

Krun threw more roots into the fire: she had not expected guests for dinner. It was typical of her son, she thought, to arrive unexpectedly and with a woman with a swollen belly. She hoped there would be enough roots to go round.

She was glad the words had not been found. She hated making small talk.

Sparg was here, in front of her. She sniffed his armpit, as was the custom when a Kronkite returned from a long journey. Barf hung back and watched the greeting ceremony. Her mouth salivated. The smell of the burning roots inflamed her hunger.

Because the words had not been found no news could be exchanged between mother and son.

Jake fell back from his computer terminal with a contented sigh. It was good, he thought, damned good. The time was right for another prehistoric novel without dialogue.

Tuesday January 21st

A letter from Bert Baxter. Almost illegible.

> Dear Lad,
> It seems a long time since I saw you. When are you coming to Leicester? I've got a few jobs that need doing. Sorry about the writing. I've got the shakes.
> Yours,
> Bertram Baxter
> P.S. Bring your toenail scissors.

Had a serious row with Bianca tonight. She accused me of:

a) Never wanting to go out
b) Excessive reading

c) Excessive writing
d) Contempt for Britain's industrial heritage
e) Farting in bed

Monday   January 27th

At last reconciled, we went to the National Film Theatre tonight and saw a film about a Japanese woman who cuts her lover's penis off. During the rest of the film, I sat with my legs tightly crossed and at intervals looked nervously across at Bianca, who was staring up at the screen and smiling.

My hair is almost long enough for a pony tail. *The Face* tells me that pony tails are becoming passé. But it may be my last chance to try one. So I am going for it. Savage has been boasting that he has had his for five years.

Bianca has bought a secondhand electric typewriter and is typing *Lo!* She has already presented me with seventy-eight beautifully laid-out pages. It is amazing how much a novel is improved by being typed. I should have taken Mr John Tydeman's advice years ago.

Wednesday   January 29th

U.K. heterosexual Aids cases rose by fifty per cent last year. I gave this information to Bianca as we walked to 'Savages' early this evening. She went very quiet.

I had to wait ages outside the bathroom tonight to clean my teeth. Eventually Norman came out and apologised for the new scorch marks on the frame of the mirror. He has been *told* not to practise in there.

When I got back to our room, I found Bianca reading a pamphlet written by the Terence Higgins Trust.

I said flippantly, 'Who's Terence Higgins when he's at home?'

'He's dead,' she said, softly. The pamphlet was about Aids.

Bianca broke down and confessed that in 1990 she had had an affair with a man called Brian Boxer, who in turn confessed to her that in 1979 he'd had an affair with a bisexual woman called Diane Tripp. I shall ring the Terence Higgins Trust Helpline in the morning and ask for help.

Saturday February 1st

The first twenty-two chapters of *Lo! The Flat Hills of My Homeland* are now a pile of 197 pages of neat typescript. I keep picking it up and walking round the room with it in my arms. I can't afford to get it photocopied, not at ten pence a page. Who do I know in London who has access to a photocopier?

> Flat 6
> Brenda's Patisserie
> Old Compton Street
> London

Dear John,
I have taken your advice and revised *Lo! The Flat Hills of My Homeland*. I have also employed the services of a professional typist and you will be pleased to see that my manuscript now consists of twenty-two chapters in typewritten form. I consider that, when completed, *Lo! The Flat Hills of My Homeland* will be eminently suitable for being read aloud on the radio, possibly as part of your Classic Serials series.

As you can see, I have enclosed my MS and entrust it into your care. However, I still need to make several minor changes. Would it be too much trouble for you to photocopy the hundred and ninety-seven pages and send a copy to me at the above address?

Thanking you in advance,
Yours as ever,
Adrian Mole

Tuesday February 4th

I walked to Broadcasting House this morning. As I struggled to push the big metal doors open, a gaggle of autograph hunters rushed towards me. I reached inside my jacket for my felt tip, but before I could extract it, I saw them surrounding Alan Freeman, the aged D.J. I pushed through them and entered the hallowed reception area of the British Broadcasting Corporation, watched by the stern-looking security staff. I walked up to the reception desk and joined the short queue.

In the space of four minutes, I saw famous people galore: Delia Smith, Robert Robinson, Ian Hislop, Bob Geldof, Annie Lennox, Roy Hattersley, etc., etc. Most of them were being seen off the premises by young women called Caroline.

Eventually the blonde receptionist said, 'Can I help you?' And I said, 'Yes. Could you please make sure that Mr John Tydeman receives this parcel? It is most urgent.'

She scribbled something on the jiffy bag which contained my letter and the manuscript of *Lo! The Flat Hills of My Homeland* and threw it into a wire basket.

I thanked her, turned to go and bumped into Victor Meldrew, who plays the grumpy bloke in *One Foot in the Grave*! I apologised and he said, 'How kind.' He is much taller than he looks on television. When I got back to the room I told Bianca that I had been chatting to Victor Meldrew. I think she was quite impressed.

Wednesday   February 5th

We both woke early this morning, but we didn't make love as usual. We had a shower and got dressed in silence. We went downstairs and had croissants and cappuccino in Brenda's Patisserie and listened to the gossip about the demise of the British film industry. Then, at 10.45 a.m., we paid our bill and walked to the clinic in Neal Street. (We forked out one pound, forty pence to the various beggars who met us on the way.)

We were counselled separately by a very empathetic woman called Judith. She pointed out that, should our tests prove positive, it wouldn't necessarily mean that we would develop full-blown Aids. After seeing Judith, we went for a drink in a pub in Carnaby Street to discuss our options:

    a) Have the test and know the worst
    b) Not to have the test and suspect the worst

We decided to sleep on it.

Thursday   February 6th

We have both decided to have the test and have pledged to care for each other until the day we die. Whatever the outcome.

Saturday   February 8th

Mr Britten, the greengrocer who supplies 'Savages' with fruit and vegetables, came into the kitchen today and told us that he is going out of business next week. He said that Savage owes him seven hundred pounds in unpaid bills. I was outraged, but Mr Britten said defeatedly that Savage is only one of his many bad debtors. He said, 'If the Bank'd give me another two weeks I'd be all right, but the bastards won't.'

I made him a cup of tea and listened to him ranting on about interest charges and Norman Lamont. I think he felt slightly better by the time he left to make his next delivery.

I rang my mother to tell her about my conversation with Victor Meldrew and found that she has also been seeing a counsellor. A debt counsellor. I have been wondering for some time now how she has been paying her mortgage. Now I know. She hasn't. She has received a legal notice from the Building Society, informing her that the house where I spent my childhood is to be repossessed on March 16th. She begged me not to tell the other members of the family. She is hoping that something will turn up to avert disaster.

I didn't tell her that I have got one thousand, one hundred and eleven pounds in the Market Harborough Building Society. But I did say that Bianca and I would come to Leicester tomorrow. She sounded pathetically grateful.

Sunday   February 9th

When we got to St Pancras Station, Bianca told me to look up.

'You are looking at one of the largest unsupported arch structures in the whole world,' she said. 'Isn't it beautiful?'

'Quite honestly, Bianca,' I said, 'all I can see is a dirty, scruffy roof covered in pigeon shit.'

'It was stupid of me to ask you to look at something further than your own nose,' she said, and stormed onto the train, leaving me to carry our overnight bags.

I'm always forgetting that Bianca is a qualified engineer. She doesn't look like one and since I've known her, she's only ever worked as a shop assistant and a waitress. She applies for at least two engineering jobs a week, but has yet to be called for an interview. She is considering calling herself 'Brian Dartington' on her c.v.

The ticket inspector forgot to punch our three-monthly returns, so our journey to Leicester cost us nothing. But any feelings of happy triumph vanished as we got into the house. My mother was putting on a brave front, but I could tell she was inwardly distraught – at one point, she had one cigarette in her mouth, another in the ashtray and another burning on the edge of the kitchen window sill. I asked her how she'd got into such terrible debt.

She whispered, 'Martin needed the fees to finish his degree course. I borrowed a thousand pounds from a finance company, at an interest rate of twenty-four point seven per cent. Two weeks later, I lost my job with Group Five – somebody grassed on me and told them I was forty-eight.' I asked her to tell me the full extent of her indebtedness. She brought out unpaid bills of every description and colour. I urged her to tell Muffet the true nature of their financial situation, but she became almost hysterical and said, 'No, no, he *must* finish his engineering degree.'

I seem to be surrounded by engineers. Bianca informed my mother that she too was a qualified engineer.

I said jokingly, 'Yes, but she has not built so much as a Lego tower since she left university.'

To my amazement, Bianca took great exception to my harmless joke and left the room, looking tearful.

My mother said, 'You tactless sod!' and followed her into the garden.

I sat at the kitchen table, braced myself, and wrote three cheques: to Fat Eddie's Loan Co. (two hundred and seventy-one pounds); to the Co-op Dairy (thirty-six pounds, forty-nine pence); to Cherry's Newsagent (seventy-four pounds, eighty-one pence). I know it does not solve my mother's housing problem, but at least she can answer her front door now without being hounded by local creditors.

When Martin came back from Grandma's (where he is in the middle of replacing her two-pin sockets with three-pin ones),

I introduced him to Bianca. Within seconds, they were bonded. They talked non-stop about St Pancras Station and unsupported arch structures. It is some time since I saw Bianca so animated. They sat next to each other at the dinner table and volunteered to wash and dry afterwards.

I helped Rosie with her English homework essay, 'A Day in the Life of a Dolphin'. I then went into the kitchen and found Bianca and Muffet droning on about the St Pancras Station Hotel and its architect, Sir George Gilbert Scott.

I interrupted them and informed Bianca that I was going to bed. She hardly looked up; just muttered, 'Okay, I'll be up soon.'

The spare bedroom was full of Rosie's hideous, fluorescent My Little Pony models.

Monday   February 10th

I have no idea what time Bianca came up last night. She must have got into bed beside me without waking me up. All I know is that Muffet and my mother are not speaking and that I am utterly miserable.

11.30 p.m. Worked on *Chapter Twenty-Three: Conundrum.*

> Jake sat in Alma's, the patisserie favoured by the intelligentsia, and scribbled on his A4 pad. Night and day, he worked on his novel. He was already on Chapter Four.
>
> *Chapter Four: Rocks*
> Sparg crept through the lush undergrowth. He knew they were there. He heard them before he saw them. They were grunting about their mutual interest in rocks.
>
> Sparg parted a yukka plant and they were there in front of him: Moff and Barf, bathed in sunlight, tangled together. Their limbs were entwined in an intimate manner.
>
> Sparg stifled a jealous grunt and crept back towards Kronk, the settlement of his birth.

Tuesday February 11th

We get our results tomorrow. I should be agonising and reflecting on mortality, etc. But all I can think about is the way that Muffet looked at Bianca and the way that Bianca looked at Muffet when they said goodbye on Monday morning at Leicester station.

Wednesday February 12th

Judith told us that our tests are negative! We are not H.I.V. positive! We are not going to die of Aids!

However, I feel that I may well die of a broken heart. Bianca has suggested another day trip to Leicester. She claims that she is tired of London. A feeble excuse. How could anyone be tired of London? I am with Dr Johnson on this one.

Thursday February 13th

A letter has arrived from the BBC.

> Dear Adrian,
> When my secretary handed me your letter and your manu-
> script of *Lo! The Flat Hills of My Homeland* yet again, I
> thought I must be hallucinating.
> You have more cheek than a Samurai wrestler, more
> neck than a giraffe. The BBC does not run a free
> photocopying service. As to your laughable suggestion
> that your novel be read as one of our classic serials . . .
> The writers of such texts are usually dead, their
> work having outlived them. I doubt if your work will
> outlive you. I am returning the manuscript immediately.
> Owing to an administrative error, a photocopy *was* taken.
> I am sending this on to you, though with great reluctance.
> You really must not bother me again.
> John Tydeman

Friday February 14th

ST VALENTINE'S DAY

A disappointingly small card from Bianca. Mine to her was a thing of splendour. Large, padded, expensive, and in a box tied with a ribbon.

Savage is in a clinic for drug and alcohol abuse. Luigi went to see him on Sunday and said that Savage was playing ping-pong with a fifteen-year-old crack addict from Leeds.

Saturday   February 15th

Bianca is going to Leicester for the day on Monday, to see my mother. I wish I could go with her, but I am now working a sixteen-hour day, seven days a week. Somebody has to keep my mother out of prison, and I am now the only person in our family who has a proper job.

My duties at 'Savages' now include the preparation of vegetables. It is tedious work, made more difficult by the obsessive attitude of Roberto, the chef. He insists on uniformity of vegetable length and width. I have to keep a tape measure in my apron pocket.

Sunday   February 16th

It is now seven days and nights since Bianca and I made love. It is not only the sex I miss. It isn't the sex. It really isn't only the sex. I miss holding her and smelling her hair and stroking her skin. I wish that I could talk to her about how I feel. But I can't, I just can't. I really can't. I've tried, but I just can't. I held her hand in bed tonight, but it didn't count. She was asleep.

Monday   February 17th

Before I went to work at 6.30 a.m., I wrote a note and left it propped against the bowl of hyacinths on the table.

> Darling Bianca,
> Please talk to me about our relationship. I am unable
> to initiate a discussion. All I can say to you is that I love
> you. I know something is wrong between us, but I don't
> know how to address it.
>   Love, forever,
>   Adrian

Bianca was very kind to me early this evening. She assured

me that nothing has changed regarding her feelings towards me. But she was talking to me on the telephone from Leicester. She has arranged to stay another day, to help my mother.

When I got home from work at 11.30 p.m., I re-read the note, which was still on the table, and then tore it up and threw it down the lavatory. It took three full flushes before it disappeared completely.

Tuesday February 18th

I was very tired last night, but was unable to sleep, so I got out of bed, got dressed, and went for a walk. Soho never sleeps. It exists for people like me: the lonely, the lovesick, the outsiders. When I got home I read Dostoievsky's *The Humiliated and Insulted*.

Wednesday February 19th

The gods are not exactly smiling on our family. Mrs Bellingham has sacked my father and kicked him out of her bed. She was outraged to find out that my father had been selling her security lights for half price in low-life pubs. He is back living with Grandma. I only know this because Grandma rang me at work, complaining that my mother owes her fifty pounds from last December. Grandma needs the money because she is going to Egypt with Age Concern in June and needs to pay the deposit next week.

I pointed out to Grandma that she has got substantial savings in a high interest bank account. Couldn't she withdraw fifty pounds? Grandma pointed out that the bank requires a month's notice of withdrawal. She said, 'I'm not prepared to lose the interest.'

I casually asked Grandma if she had seen anything of Bianca. She casually answered that she had seen Bianca and Muffet on the top deck of a number twenty-nine bus, heading towards the town. She threw in a few details. They were laughing. Bianca was holding a bunch of freesias (her favourite flowers). And Muffet looked 'happier than I've ever seen him'. There was a twanging noise as she leaned back in her chair by the telephone and said,

'It doesn't take an Einstein to work that one out, does it, lad?'

Thanks, Grandma, Leicester's answer to Miss sodding Marple.

Thursday February 20th

I fear the worst. Bianca is still in Leicester. I received a brochure this morning from an organisation called the Faxos Institute. They were offering me a holistic holiday on the Greek island of Faxos, complete with courses in creative writing, dream workshops, finding your voice and stress management. One photograph in the brochure showed happy, tanned holidaymakers scoffing green foodstuffs at long tables under blue skies. Close examination with a magnifying glass showed the foodstuffs to be made up of lettuce and courgettes with a bit of what looked like cheese thrown in. There were bottles of retsina on the tables, vases of flowers and rough-hewn loaves of bread.

Another photograph showed a beach and a pine forest and the bamboo hut accommodation spread over a hillside. It looked truly idyllic. I turned a page and saw that Angela Hacker, the novelist, playwright and television personality, was 'facilitating' the writing course for the first two weeks in April. I have not read her books or seen her plays, but I have seen her on the television programme *Through the Keyhole*. She has certainly got a gracious home, though I remember being struck at the time by the amazing amount of alcohol in evidence. There were bottles in every room. Loyd Grossman made a quip about it at the time, something about 'sauce for the goose'. The studio audience laughed itself stupid.

I closed the brochure with a sigh. Two weeks on Faxos talking about my novel with Angela Hacker would be paradise, but I can't possibly afford it. My Building Society reserves are running low. I'm down to my last thousand.

Saturday February 22nd

Bianca rang the restaurant at lunchtime and said that she would be catching the 7.30 a.m. train from Leicester tomorrow and would be arriving at St Pancras at around 9.00 a.m. Her voice sounded strange. I asked her if she'd got a sore throat. She replied that she'd been 'doing a lot of talking'. Every fibre of me longs for her, especially the bits around my loins.

Sunday   February 23rd

I was on the platform when the train came in and saw Bianca jump onto the platform. I ran towards her, holding a bunch of daffodils I'd bought from a stall outside the Underground on Oxford Street. Then, to my surprise, I saw Martin Muffet step down from the train, carrying two large suitcases. He put them down on the platform and put his arm around Bianca's slim shoulders.

Bianca said, 'I'm sorry, Adrian.'

Muffet said, 'So am I.'

To be quite honest, I didn't know what to say.

I turned away, leaving the two engineers under the engineering miracle of St Pancras Station and made my way back to Old Compton Street on foot. I don't know what happened to the daffodils, but I hadn't got them when I arrived home.

Monday   February 24th

Chapter Twenty-Four: Oblivion

Jake slipped the hose over the exhaust pipe and checked that it was properly connected. Then he put the other end of the hose through the side window of the car. He took a long, last look at the glorious vista of the Lake District panorama spread beneath him. 'How glorious life is,' he said, aloud, to the wind. All around him the daffodils nodded their agreement. Jake took his portable electric razor from his toiletry bag and proceeded to shave. He had always been vain and he was particularly keen to look good as a corpse. His bristles flew into the wind and became as one with the earth. Jake splashed on Obsession, his favourite after-shave lotion. Then, his toilette completed, he climbed into the car and switched on the engine.

As the fumes filled the inside of the car, Jake ruminated on his life. He had visited four continents and bedded some of the world's most beautiful women. He had recovered the Ashes for England. He had climbed Everest backwards, and found the definitive source of the Nile. Nobody could say that his life had been without interest. But, without Regina, the girl he loved, he did not want to live. As Jake slipped into oblivion, the needle on the petrol gauge turned to 'E'. Which would run out first, Jake's oxygen supply, or Jake's petrol . . . ?

Tuesday February 25th

Got the courage up to ring my mother. My father answered. He said that he has moved back to live with my mother 'on a temporary basis' until she has recovered from the immediate shock of the Bianca/Muffet affair. Apparently, she is too ill to leave her bed and look after Rosie.

He asked how I had taken it.

I said, 'Oh me, I'm fine,' and then big, fat tears rolled down my cheeks and into the electronic workings of the telephone handset. My father kept saying, down the phone, 'There, there, lad. There, there, don't cry, lad,' in a tender voice that I don't remember him using before.

Roberto the chef came and stood at my side and wiped the tears away with his apron. Eventually, after promising to keep in touch, I said goodbye to my father. For years I have thought of him as a feckless fool, but I now see that I have misjudged him.

When I got back to the room, I found that Bianca had taken all her personal belongings, including the photograph of Isambard Kingdom Brunel.

Wednesday February 26th

I went to a place called Ed's Diner at lunchtime today and had a hot dog, fries, a Becks beer and a mug of filter coffee. I asked for a glass for my beer and then noticed that the other men of my age were swigging it from the bottle, so I pushed my glass away surreptitiously and did as they did. I sat at a high stool at the counter in front of a mini-jukebox. Each selection cost five pence. I selected only one record, but I played it three times.

I used to be able to recite the lyric of 'Stand by Me' off by heart. Bianca and I used to sing along with Ben E. King when we cooked Sunday breakfast together. Our percussion instruments included: a box of household matches, a spatula, and a tin of dried lentils.

In Ed's Diner I tried to sing the words under my breath but I couldn't remember a word.

At the end of the song I was in tears. Why couldn't she have stood by me?

A man sitting on the next stool asked if there was anything he could do. I tried to compose myself, but to my absolute horror I began to sob loudly and without restraint. There were tears; there was snot; there were undignified gulpings and heavings of the shoulders. The stranger put his arm around my shoulders and asked, 'Have you had a relationship gone wrong?'

I nodded, then managed to say, in between sobs, 'Finished.'

'Same here,' he said. Then 'My name's Alan.' Alan told me that he was 'devastated' because his partner, Christopher, had fallen for another man. I ordered two more beers and then I told Alan the whole story about Bianca and Martin Muffet. Alan confessed himself to be shocked and was thoughtful enough to enquire as to my mother's feelings. I told him that I'd phoned her last night and that she'd told me that her life was over.

Alan and I have arranged to meet for a drink at 8.00 p.m. tonight. Am I now, like Blanche Dubois, dependent on the kindness of strangers?

Midnight Alan didn't turn up. I sat in the 'Coach and Horses' for over an hour, waiting for him. Perhaps he met another stranger with a more original tragic story.

I miss her. I miss her. I miss her.

Thursday   February 27th

Roberto stood over me this evening and made me eat a plate of tagliatelle with hare sauce. He said 'A woman issa woman, but food issa food.'

Perhaps it has more meaning in the original Italian.

Jake handed the envelope containing the money to the sinister man.

'Quick and clean,' he said. 'They mustn't know what hit them.'

The man grunted and left the Soho drinking den. Jake looked around him, at the tawdry, painted girls, at the bestial faces of the late night drinkers. Was it only yesterday he was in the Lake District attempting suicide? As he rose to his feet, a young prostitute attempted to procure him. He pushed her away irritably, saying, 'Get lost, baby, I've known and lost the only woman I'll ever want.'

He strode out into the vibrant Soho night, his cowboy boots tapping strangely on the murky pavement. I must get them soled and heeled tomorrow, he thought. As he passed down Old Compton Street, he looked up at the window of the flat above Alma's Patisserie. The light was still burning but he knew that by now all human life had been extinguished. He was a murderer by proxy.

Tears poured inside his heart, but his face was as it always was, hard and unforgiving and without God's blessing.

Saturday February 29th

I have informed Mr Andropolosis, the landlord, that I have taken over the tenancy, and paid him a month's rent in advance, so the room is now mine. Thank God for the end of this month. It has surely been the worst since time began.

To complete our catalogue of family misery, Grandma was admitted to hospital during the early hours of this morning with abdominal pains. I rang the hospital this afternoon and was told by the ward sister that Grandma was 'comfortable'. If this is true, then she is the only member of the family who is – the rest of us are in total misery.

Sunday March 1st

I joined my mother, father and Rosie at Grandma's hospital bedside this afternoon. It was the first time I had seen Grandma without her teeth. I was shocked at how *old* she looked.

My mother has lost weight and her eyes looked sore, as though she has been weeping constantly since Muffet upped and left her. After visiting time was over and we were trooping down the ward, my mother said bitterly: 'They're in Hounslow, staying with his brother, Andrew.'

I said, 'I don't want to know, Mum.'

My father said, 'Let it drop, Pauline.'

Rosie said, 'I'm glad he's gone. I hope he never comes back.' She held her hand up and my father took it and steered her through the big double doors at the end of the ward. As we walked alongside the hospital tower blocks, the litter swirled around our feet and I had a premonition of doom.

I almost turned back to say a proper goodbye to Grandma, but I didn't want to keep the others hanging around in the potholed car park, so I didn't. Instead, we went home and had a Marks and Spencer's roast beef dinner each. Mine was quite nice, but it wasn't a patch on the real thing cooked by my grandma. As I was compressing the dirty tin foil trays into the kitchen pedal bin, the telephone rang. It was the hospital, telling us that 'Mrs Edna May Mole passed away at 5.15 p.m.'

I tried to remember where I was *exactly* at 5.15 p.m. I worked out that I was in a B.P. petrol station, helping my father to check the pressure in his car tyres.

I haven't shed a single tear for her yet. I'm dried up inside. My heart feels like a peach stone.

Monday   March 2nd

It is a well-known fact that Grandma and my mother never got on, so nobody was prepared for the positively Mediterranean grief my mother is displaying over her mother-in-law's death: copious tears, breast-beating, etc. This morning she was lamenting, 'I owed her fifty quid' over and over again.

My father continues to astonish me with his maturity. He has dealt with all the death paperwork and haggled over the cost of the funeral with commendable efficiency.

Tuesday   March 3rd

At 10.00 p.m. I rang 'Savages' to tell them that I am staying in Leicester for the funeral on Friday afternoon. Roberto said, 'I'm glad you ring, Adrian. Your flat has been called on by burglars.' He made it sound as though burglars had been invited to tea, brought flowers and left a visiting card. There's nothing I can do tonight. The police have employed the services of a locksmith. The new key is at 'Savages'. I feel strangely calm.

Wednesday   March 4th

Train to Leicester 8.40 p.m.
They have taken everything, apart from my books, boxer shorts and an old pair of polyester trousers. How they got the bed down the stairs will probably always remain a mystery. The policeman I spoke to on the phone said, in answer to my question about the likelihood of their finding the culprits: 'You know what chance a snowball has in hell? Well, halve that. Then halve it again.' He asked if I had insurance.

I laughed scornfully and said, 'Of course not. This is Adrian Mole you're speaking to.'

I am now a man without possessions.

Thursday   March 5th

I went into Grandma's home this morning. Everything was the same as ever. My G.C.E. certificates were still there, framed on the wall. My dead grandad Albert's photograph was on the mantelpiece. The clock was still ticking. Upstairs, the linen lay folded in the cupboard and in the garden the bulbs pushed through the earth. The biscuit barrel was full of fig rolls and her second best slippers stood by her bed. Inside a kitchen cupboard, I found her Yorkshire pudding tin. She had used it for over forty years. Stupid to weep over a Yorkshire pudding tin, but I did. I then wiped it dry and replaced it in the cupboard, as she would have liked.

Friday   March 6th

GRANDMA'S FUNERAL

My mother and father, Rosie and I worked together as a team today and managed to give Grandma a good send-off. There was a respectable turnout in the church, which surprised me, because Grandma didn't encourage people to call on her. She preferred the company of Radio Four. She had been known to turn people away from her doorstep, should they be inconsiderate enough to call during the Afternoon Play.

The hymns were 'Amazing Grace' and 'Onward Christian Soldiers'. Bert Baxter sang out loudly, almost drowning the others in the congregation. For an atheist, he certainly enjoys singing in church. As I watched him, I couldn't help thinking wistfully that it should have been him who died instead of Grandma. The vicar said a lot of incredibly stupid things about Grandma being born into sin and dying in sin.

Anybody who knew Grandma knew that she was incapable of sin. She couldn't even tell a lie. When I asked her once if my spots were clearing up (I must have been about fifteen), she answered, 'No, you've still got a face like a ladybird's arse.' She occasionally used such mild profanities, but she was certainly not a sinner.

I don't like to think of her lying under the earth, alone and cold. Still, at least she was never burgled or mugged. She is safe from all that now.

* * *

The funeral tea was held at our house. My mother had been up most of the previous night, cleaning and polishing and trying to get the stains out of the lounge carpet.

My father replaced the missing light bulbs and mended the ballcock so that the lavatory flushed properly.

Tania Braithwaite came round to give her commiserations and kindly offered to defrost some vegetarian quiches she had in the freezer. She told us that Pandora had cancelled a lecture and was intending to come to the funeral tea and would be bringing six bottles of Marks and Spencer's champagne with her.

She said, 'Pandora believes in celebrating death. She sees it as a new adventure, as opposed to a rather boring ending.'

Bert Baxter had phoned to ask what time the service

started, which reminded my mother that there was no beetroot in the house. So Rosie was given a personal safety alarm and sent round to the corner shop to buy a jar from Mr Patel's shop.

At midnight, I watched my parents spreading a white table-cloth over the dining room table, which had had its leaves fully extended. As they flapped and adjusted the cloth, one at either end, I had a sudden sense of being a member of the family.

Rosie had arranged some daffodils and freesias nicely in a vase and was praised by everyone. Even the dog behaved itself. When we finally went to bed, the house looked perfect; everything was in its place and we Moles could hold our heads high. Grandma would have been proud of us.

* * *

After the funeral service, Rosie and I ran ahead of the other mourners to take the clingfilm off the sandwiches and sausage rolls.

Pandora was waiting outside the house in her car. We filled the bath with cold water and put the bottles of champagne into it to chill.

Pandora looked beautifully severe in a black tailored suit. However, I no longer felt in awe of her, so we were able to talk to each other as friends and equals. She complimented me on how well I was looking and she even praised my clothes. She fingered the lapel of my navy blue unstructured Next suit and said, 'Welcome to the nineties.'

The house soon filled up with mourners and I was kept busy circulating with glasses of champagne on a tray. At first, everyone stood around, not knowing what to say, nervous of enjoying themselves for fear of being thought disrespectful to the dead. Then Pandora broke the ice by proposing a toast to Grandma.

'To Edna Mole,' she said, lifting her glass of champagne high, 'a woman of the highest principles.'

Everyone clinked glasses and swigged back the champagne and it wasn't long before laughter broke out and I was fishing the bottles out of the bath.

My mother rummaged in the sideboard and brought out the

photograph albums. I was astonished to see a photograph of my
grandma at the age of twenty-four. She looked very dashing,
dark-haired, with a lovely figure, and was laughing and pushing
a bicycle up a hill. There was a man next to her wearing a flat
cap. He had a big moustache and his eyes were crinkled against
the sun. It was my grandad. Everybody remarked that I looked
like him.

My father took the photograph out of the album and
went into the garden and sat on Rosie's swing. After a while, I
followed him out. He handed me the photograph and said, 'I'm
an orphan, son.'

I put my hand on his shoulder, then went back inside to
find that the funeral tea had turned into a party. People were
laughing hysterically at the photographs in the album. Me at
the seaside, falling off a donkey. Me in a secondhand cub's
uniform three sizes too big. Me at six months, lying naked on
a half moon-shaped rug in front of a gas fire. Me two days
old with my grinning, young-looking parents in the maternity
hospital. On the back was written, in my mother's handwriting,
'Our darling baby, two days old'.

There was a photograph I don't remember seeing before.
It was my mother and father and my grandma and grandad.
They were sitting in deckchairs, watching me, aged about three,
playing in the sand. On the back was written: 'Yarmouth, Bank
Holiday Monday'.

Rosie said, 'Why aren't I in the photo?'

Bert Baxter said, 'Cos you 'adn't been bleedin' born, that's
why.'

At seven o'clock, Ivan Braithwaite offered to escort some
of my grandma's elderly neighbours back to their pensioners'
bungalows while they and he could still walk.

The rest of us carried on until eleven o'clock. Tania Braithwaite, who has been vegetarian for nine years, cracked and ate
a sausage roll and then another.

My mother and father danced together to 'You've Lost
That Loving Feeling'. You couldn't have slid a ruler between
them.

Pandora and I watched them dancing. She said, 'So they're
back together again, are they?'

'I hope so,' I said, looking at Rosie.

As I said before, it was a good send-off.

Monday   March 9th

Old Compton Street

I am back in my room with only my books and boxer shorts for company. I have given the trousers away to a young man selling *The Big Issue*. I made a pillow out of my underwear and slept on the floor. I have often wondered what it would be like to be a celibate monk in a bare cell. Now, thanks to burglary and desertion, I know.

I went into 'Savages' to help clean the kitchen. Savage himself was there, released from the alcohol abuse unit and looking fit and athletic and sipping on a glass of mineral water. He commiserated with me on my various losses and said that there was some old furniture in the attic above the restaurant that I could have.

'Just help yourself, kid,' he said.

I can't get used to this new, kind, philanthropic Savage. I keep thinking he must be Savage's long lost twin brother, recently returned from a missionary station in Amazonia.

My room is now furnished with rococo style banquettes and fag-stained *faux* marble tables. Stuff that was obviously thrown upstairs when Savage took over the restaurant. I now sleep on two banquettes pushed together. I have angels at my head and cherubs at my feet. Roberto gave me some cutlery and crockery and kitchen utensils. Most of my fellow workers brought something to work with them this morning, to donate to the Adrian Mole Disaster Fund. I cook on a ring fuelled by a gas canister and I read by a mock chandelier, both donated by Luigi.

Wednesday   March 11th

I rang home this morning. My father is still there, living in sin with my mother. My mother told me that Bianca and Muffet are intending to set up an engineering partnership called 'Dartington and Muffet'.

I cannot bear the thought of Muffet's bony fingers touching Bianca's lovely pale skin.

I cannot bear it.

Thursday   March 12th

Chapter Twenty-Five: Resurgence
Jake sat down at the *faux* marble table and began to
write another chapter of his novel, *Sparg from Kronk*.

Chapter Five: Green Shoots
Sparg missed his woman, Barf. There was a part
of him that would never be reconciled to her loss.

It was springtime. Green shoots showed through the
earth. Sparg left his hut and went outside. He was glad
to be outside, for the hut was damp and the damp was
rising fast.

Sparg needed a woman, but the only woman in
sight was Krun, his mother. Though her face was
wrinkled, her thighs were inviting. But it was forbidden
by Kronkian law to take your own mother, even if she
agreed.

Sparg walked aimlessly up a small hill and then
walked aimlessly down. He was bored. There was
firewood to collect, but he was sick of collecting firewood. It did not challenge his intellect. He grunted in
despair and wished it were possible to communicate
with his fellow Kronkians. It was just his luck, he
thought, to be born in prehistoric times.

If only there was *language*, grunted Sparg internally . . .

to be continued

Jake fell back. The intensity of the writing had left him
drained and pale. He left his room and walked to Wilde's,
his favourite restaurant, where he was greeted by Mario.

'Longa tima noa see, Mr Westmorland.'

'Hi, Mario. My usual table, please, and my usual bottle,
well chilled, and I'll have my usual starter, usual main
course and usual pudding.'

'And for your aperitif, Mr Westmorland?' purred Mario.

'The usual,' barked Jake.

I've got to finish *Lo! The Flat Hills of My Homeland* soon, but I can't do that until Jake has finished writing *Sparg from Kronk*. I wish he would hurry up.

Friday   March 13th

More businesses are closing around us. Every day, the boards go up at shop and restaurant windows. Every night, I pray that 'Savages' stays financially viable. I need my job. I'm aware that I'm being exploited, but at least I have a reason to get up in the morning, unlike three and a half million of my fellow citizens.

Grandma left my father three thousand and ninety pounds in her will, so my mother is not going to have her house repossessed. This is truly joyous news. It means that I won't have to break into my Building Society savings. I couldn't have seen her thrown onto the street. At least, I don't think I could.

Saturday   March 14th

I received the following message when I got to work this morning. It was written on the back of a paper napkin. 'Forgot G. Left 500.' Nobody knew what it meant or who had taken the message.

Monday   March 16th

Received another brochure from the Faxos Institute. Why are they mailing me so assiduously? Who has put them on to me? I don't know any holistic types. I'm not even a vegetarian and I swear by paracetamol.

I went to the National Gallery today, but it brought back painful memories of B., so I went back to Soho and paid two pounds to watch a fat girl with spots remove her bra and knickers through a peephole. I *watched* her through a peephole. She didn't remove her underclothes through a peephole.

Query: Are there night classes in syntax?

Tuesday   March 17th

I ran out of toilet paper last night and reached for the Faxos Institute brochure to help me out of my emergency, when something about Angela Hacker's face made me pause. It seemed to say, 'Come to me, Adrian.' Her face is nothing to write home about, in fact it's nothing to write *anywhere* about.

I put the brochure down and picked up the *Evening Standard* instead. It has far better absorbency qualities.

11.45 p.m. Can't sleep for St Patrick's Day revellers, so have idly filled in the booking form for the first two weeks in April at the Faxos Institute in Greece.

Thursday   March 19th

Idly filled in a cheque made out to 'Faxos Institute', but I was only trying out a new pen. I couldn't possibly afford the time off work, or the money.

10.00 p.m. The full message was: 'Forgot to tell you Grandma has left you five hundred pounds, love, Dad.' Luigi, who had been away from the restaurant with food poisoning, returned today and congratulated me on 'Alla money ya got'. Naturally, I looked at him blankly. Confusion abounded for some minutes and then came the glorious realisation, which we celebrated with a bottle of corked Frascati.

Saturday   March 21st

The newly benign Savage has agreed to give me two weeks' leave (without pay). I posted my booking form this morning and this afternoon I bought some swimming trunks from a shop that was closing down in the Charing Cross Road. I can't wait to feel the warm Aegean sea on my body.

Worked on *Lo!* with Angela Hacker in mind.

> Jake opened his manuscript book. The ivory handmade paper looked enticing. He took his Mont Blanc pen in his hand and began to write.
>
> 'Sorry, darling,' he said to the glorious example of English womanhood who sprawled opposite him, showing her knickers, 'but the Muse is upon me.'
>
> Then he lowered his handsome head and was at once in Kronk, the home of his hero, Sparg.
>
> Sparg grunted, recognising the hated form of his father

in the darkness. His father grunted back. Sparg threw a pebble from one hand to the other. Why hadn't something been invented to pass the hours of darkness before bed, he wondered. Something like a game such as cards, he wondered. He went back into his hut and pushed the animal skins listlessly around on his bed. He was cold at night without a woman. He determined that he would get up early the next morning and find one and bring her home to Kronk.

Thursday   March 26th

I bought a short-sleeved shirt and a pair of Bermuda shorts from a stall in Berwick Street market. I have never worn shorts since reaching adulthood.

A new Adrian Mole is emerging from the ashes.

Savage turned up drunk and disorderly at the restaurant and proceeded to fire Luigi, Roberto and the whole of the kitchen staff apart from me. He said, 'You can stay, Adrian. You're a fucking loser, like me.'

He has promoted me to *Maître d'*, a position I do not want and cannot do.

Luigi and Roberto sat in the kitchen, smoking and talking in Italian. They didn't seem too concerned. Meanwhile, dressed in Luigi's suit, I was forced to fawn over customers, show them to their seats and pretend to be interested in their requirements. Savage sat at the bar, shouting out the biographical details of his customers as they came in. As one respectable-looking middle-aged couple entered, he yelled: 'Well, if it isn't Mr and Mrs Wellington. He's wearing a toupée and she's paid three thousand pounds for those perky looking titties.'

Instead of going straight back out, or thumping him on the side of his drunken head, Mr and Mrs Wellington grinned and allowed me to show them to table number six. Perhaps they are proud of their artificial attributes. As my recently dead grandma would say, 'There's nowt so strange as folk, especially London folk.'

Poor Grandma. She never went to London in her life.

For the past four days, I have been unable to write a word. The thought of Angela Hacker reading my manuscript has totally inhibited me. However, tonight I achieved a breakthrough.

> He had writer's block. For over five hours he stared down at the mockingly empty page. His publisher was calling hourly. The printing presses were waiting, but still he could not finish his book. Jake looked out of the window, hoping for inspiration. The New York skyline stretched away into infinity . . .
>
> 'Infinity!' shouted Jake, excitedly, and he began to work on his novel, *Sparg from Kronk*.

> Sparg had wandered far from Kronk and was standing on a high headland, looking in wonderment at a strange watery mass and a blue line ahead of him. Without knowing it (because there was no language), Sparg was marvelling over the sea and the far distant horizon. Sparg growled and began to descend the headland. He would walk to the far blue line, he thought. It would be something to do. Sparg thought this because there was as yet no swimming . . .

Received confirmation from Faxos Institute that I have a place on the Writers' Course. I am terrified.

Friday   March 27th

Luigi has been reinstated and I am safely back in the kitchen, thank God. Roberto has been allowing me to watch him at work. For most of my life, I have been denied a proper food education. There was never anything to learn from my mother; she stopped cooking real food soon after reading *The Female Eunuch*. Though, ironically, the author of that seminal tome, Ms Germaine Greer, is a renowned cook and dinner party giver.

Thanks to Roberto's kindness, I can now cook pasta '*al dente*' and make a basic sponge cake and I've almost cracked making watercress soup. I now spring from my double banquettes in the morning, eager to get to work.

Plane tickets arrived today.

A new girl started work as a waitress at 'Savages' this evening. Her name is Jo Jo and she is from Nigeria. She is studying Art at St Martin's. She is taller than anybody else in the restaurant.

Her hair is braided with hundreds of tiny beads. She rattles when she walks. Her mother is something big in the Nigerian tractor industry.

Saturday   March 28th

Made a *tower* of profiteroles today. Roberto said: 'Congratulations, Adriana! The chocolate icing issa perfection.'

Jo Jo tasted the first one and pronounced it to be 'delectable'. Luigi happened to have his polaroid camera with him, so he photographed me and the tower and Jo Jo. I have pinned the photograph on my wall. I look quite handsome.

Sunday   March 29th

I was still in bed at midday when there was a knock on the door. I never have visitors, so I was a little alarmed. I put my ear to the door, but all I could hear was a peculiar rattling noise. I eventually opened the door, but I kept the security chain on. I was delighted to see Jo Jo through the crack.

She smiled at me and said that she was going to the Tate Gallery.

'Do you want to come?' she asked.

I slipped the chain off and invited her in. She walked around the room and commented on how tidy it was. She stopped at the table where my manuscript lay in its transparent folder and said, 'So this is your book.'

She touched it reverently. 'I would like to read it one day.'

'When it's finished,' I said.

I made her a cup of Nescafé and then excused myself and went into the bathroom to wash and change.

I looked at myself in the washbasin mirror. Something had happened to my face. I no longer looked like John Major.

Jo Jo likes walking, so we walked to the Tate. I was proud to be seen with such a stunning looking woman. I asked her about Nigeria and she spoke about her country with obvious love. She is a Yoruba and comes from Abeokuta.

She asked me about my family and I told her about the tangled web of relationships, the break-ups and the reconciliations.

She laughed and said, 'To work out the relationships in my

family, you would need an extremely sophisticated computer.'

I had never been to the Tate, but Jo Jo knew it well. She guided me round and made me look at a few of her favourite paintings – all depicting people, I noticed. We looked at paintings by Paula Rego, Vanessa Bell and Matisse, and a piece of sculpture by Ghisha Koenig called 'The Machine Minders', and then she insisted that we leave before we got bored and our feet started to ache.

As we were going down the steps, Jo Jo asked if I would like to have tea at her flat in Battersea.

I said, 'I'd love to.' We crossed the road and stood at the bus stop, but then, on impulse, I flagged down a black cab and we rode to her flat in style.

She lives on the top floor of a mansion block. Every room is full of her paintings. Many of the paintings are nude self-portraits, in which she has depicted herself in many colours, including green, pink, purple, blue and yellow.

I asked her if she was making a statement about her colour. 'No,' she laughed. 'But I would get bored only using blacks and browns.'

We ate scones and drank Earl Grey tea and talked non-stop: about 'Savages'; Nigerian politics; cats; one of her art teachers, who is going mad; Cecil Parkinson; the price of paint brushes; Vivaldi; our star signs – she is Leo (but on the cusp of Cancer); and her girls' boarding school in Surrey, where she lived from the age of eleven until she got expelled at sixteen for climbing on the roof of the chapel in a protest against the lousy food.

Over a glass of cheap wine, we discussed trees; Matisse; Moscow; Russian politics; our favourite cakes; the use of umbrellas; cabbage; and the Royal Family. She is a republican, she said.

Over a final glass of wine and a plate of bread and cheese, I talked to her about my grandmother, my mother, Pandora, Sharon, Megan, Leonora, Cassandra and Bianca. 'You're carrying a lot of baggage,' Jo Jo said.

We parted at 10.30 p.m. with a friendly handshake.

Before she closed the door, I asked how old she was.

'Twenty-four,' she said. 'Goodnight.'

Monday   March 30th

I ran out of 'Savages' during my break time and bought Ambre Solaire (Factor 8), espadrilles, sleeveless tee shirts, three more pairs of shorts and sixteen thousand drachmas.

I worked on the book late into the night. I am nervous about Angela Hacker's opinion. Added more descriptive words to *Lo! The Flat Hills of My Homeland* and took out more descriptive words from *Sparg from Kronk*.

Tuesday   March 31st

The staff arranged a small *bon voyage* party in the kitchen after the restaurant closed at lunchtime. I was very touched. Roberto cooked kebabs and arranged an authentic Greek salad in my honour. Jo Jo bought two bottles of retsina earlier in the day and we all clinked glasses and swore eternal friendship. Then Savage came in, complaining that Luigi had forgotten to add V.A.T. to somebody's bill, so the party broke up. Jo Jo is good at packing, she said. She offered to come and help me.

I laid my clothes, toiletry bag and manuscript out on my bed before proceeding to pack, and then realised that the burglars had taken my suitcase.

Jo Jo ran to Berwick Street market and bought one of those man-made fibre striped bags, the type that refugees have on the television news. Once I was packed, I debated with Jo Jo on whether or not to take a warm coat with me. She said I ought to, but I decided not to. Instead, I slung a cotton sweater around my shoulders. Everybody has said that Greece is warm in April. My legs look very white at the moment in my shorts, but by the time I return, they will be gloriously tanned.

Dear Jo Jo,

For the first time in my life, there is nobody to wish me a
Happy Birthday. I am now twenty-five years old. Which is a
millstone in anybody's life. Do I still qualify to be called a
'Young British Novelist'? I hope so.

Other participants in the Faxos Institute course are
swirling around downstairs in the hotel lobby, chatting
easily to each other. I fled back into the lift when I saw
them, and went up to the roof terrace, but Angela Hacker
was up there, smoking a cigarette and looking moodily at
the Acropolis in the far distance. She is skinny and dresses
in white clothes. She was weighed down by ethnic silver
jewellery.

I don't know when the photograph of her in the brochure was taken, but in life she looks at least forty-eight.
Obviously past it, sexually and artistically.

I didn't thank you properly for that afternoon in the
Tate. I keep thinking about the pictures. I particularly
liked those painted by that Portuguese woman, Paula
something.

　　All best wishes,
　　　　Adrian

Ferry
Friday April 3rd

Dear Mum and Dad,
I am writing this on the first ferry, which is taking us to
where we catch the second ferry to Faxos. Angela Hacker
and most of the twelve members of the writers' group are
already in the bar. The majority of them smoke. You would
probably get along famously with them, Mum. The other,
more holistic, holidaymakers are looking over the side of
the ship, taking photographs or swapping aromatherapy
recipes. I am keeping to myself. I don't want to lumber
myself with a hastily-made 'friend' and spend the next
fortnight getting rid of him or her. It has just started to
rain. I will have to stop now and go inside.
    Love from your son,
        Adrian

Ferry
Friday April 3rd
4.00 p.m.

Dear Jo Jo,
There has been torrential rain for the whole of the three-
hour crossing. I am wearing my cotton sweater, but am still
cold. I now wish I'd followed your advice and brought a
coat with me.
    Angela Hacker has been falling down in the bar. The
sea *is* choppy, but I think her lack of balance is due more
to the copious amounts of retsina she is throwing down her
neck. My fellow writers have been laughing non-stop since
boarding the ferry. Some private joke, no doubt. I have not
yet introduced myself to them.

Bamboo Hut Number Six
8.00 p.m.

The wind is whistling through the slats of my hut. Outside,
the sky is grey and dotted with storm clouds. Supper was
eaten in the open air, under a 'roof' of palm fronds. Not
surprisingly, the ratatouille was cold.
    I can hear Angela Hacker coughing from here, though

her hut is at least two hundred yards further down the rocky hill.

There was a community meeting at eight o'clock, where the permanent staff and the facilitators introduced themselves and their work. The meeting was held in what they call here the 'Magic Ring', which is on the very top of the hill. The Magic Ring is a concrete base, surrounded by a low wall and covered in the usual palm frond and bamboo roof. There is nothing magical looking about it.

I was most concerned to hear Ms Hacker describe her course as 'Writing for Pleasure'. I get no pleasure from writing. Writing is a serious business, like painting.

There is a man here who wears his hair like yours. I saw him on the headland, looking out to sea. From a distance he looked like you. My heart did a backflip.

My hut is next to the hen-coop. A goat has just put its head inside my hut and a donkey is braying somewhere in the pine woods. If Noah's Ark was washed up on the beach, I wouldn't be surprised.

> Best wishes,
> Adrian

> Faxos
> Sunday April 5th

Dear Pan,
You asked me to let you know how the Faxos course was, so I'll tell you about the first day.

The writers collected on the terrace at 11.15 a.m. I sat upwind, away from the cigarette smoke. At 11.30 a.m. Angela Hacker had still not appeared, so a man called Clive, who had seven boils on his neck, was sent to her hut. She eventually showed up at noon and apologised for having overslept. She then rambled on for an hour and fifteen minutes about 'Truth' and 'Narrative thrust' and 'developing an original voice'.

At 1.15 p.m. she sprang to her feet and said, 'Okay, that's it for the day. Write a poem including the word "Greece". Be prepared to read it aloud at 11.15 tomorrow morning.'

She then headed for the bamboo bar, where she stayed for most of the day. When I'd written my poem, I went in for a cup of tea and heard her talking about your college in Oxford.

I asked her if she knew you and she said she had met you at Jack Cavendish's house a few times, 'before Jack left his third wife,' she said.

I said, 'It's a small world.'

'Try not to use clichés, darling,' she said.

She's a strange woman.

All the best from,
    Adrian

                 Faxos
          Monday April 6th

Dear Rosie,

I hope you like this postcard of the cheerful donkey. There is something about its daft expression that reminds me of the dog.

I have sent you a poem I was forced to write about Greece. It's time you started to take an interest in cultural matters. There is more to life than Nintendo games.

Love from your brother,
    Adrian

Oh Greece, ancient cultured land
You wrap around my heart just like
An old elastic band.
Your hag-like women pensioners
Clad in clothes of black,
Are they unaware of all the services they lack?
Will they be content to watch
The donkey with its load?
Won't they want a vehicle to
Drive along the road?

Faxos
Tuesday April 7th

Dear Baz,

I am here on Faxos with Angela Hacker, whom I understand you know quite well. She and I hit it off immediately and she has invited me to stay at her place in Gloucestershire when we get back. I may be able to make the odd weekend, but I am currently doing research in a restaurant kitchen in Soho for my next book, *The Chopper*, so will not be able to stay for a couple of weeks, as she would like.

The reason I am writing is to say that I hope there are no hard feelings any more over the Sharon Bott affair, because we are likely to be moving in the same circles soon and I would rather there were no acrimonious feelings between us.

Congratulations on finally getting to number one!
Cheers,
Your old friend,
        Adrian Mole

Faxos
Wednesday April 8th

Dear John Tydeman,

As you cannot fail to see, if you have noticed the postmark, I am on the Greek island of Faxos. I am a member of a writers' course being facilitated by Angela Hacker (she sends you her love).

She asked us to write the first scene of a radio play, which is something I have never attempted to do before.

I thought you might be interested to read what I have written. I would be more than willing to finish it, if you thought it had merit.

I shall be back in London at 3.00 p.m. on the 15th April, if you would like to talk to me face to face.

On second thoughts, the 16th would be more convenient for me. I shall probably need to rest after my journey.

Here is how the play opens:

The Cucumber Sandwich
A Play for Radio by Adrian Mole

A room in a wealthy house. A game of tennis can be heard through the french windows. Tea is poured. A spoon rattles in a cup.

LADY ELEANOR: A cucumber sandwich, Edwin?
EDWIN: Don't try to fob me off with your bourgeois ideas of gentility. I know the truth!
LADY ELEANOR (*gasps*): No! Surely not! You don't know the secret I have kept for forty years!
EDWIN (*contemptuously*): Yes, I do. The servant girl, Millie, told me.

A bell rings.

MILLIE: You rang, mum? Sorry to keep you, only I was 'elpin' cook with Master Edwin's twenty-first birthday cake.
LADY ELEANOR: You are dismissed, Millie. You have blabbed my secret.
MILLIE: What secret? Oh! The one about your being born a man?

To be continued

I do not wish to prejudice you in any way, but after I had finished reading this text, there was a stunned silence from my fellow writers. Angela's only comment was, 'You should have spun the secret out until the last scene of the play.'

Good advice, I think.

Anyway, I hope you enjoy *The Cucumber Sandwich*.

Yours,

With best wishes,

Adrian Mole

Faxos
Thursday April 9th

Dear Jo Jo,
The sun has shone for two days now and has turned
Faxos into Paradise. The colours are breathtaking: the
sea is peacock blue, the grass is peppermint green and
the wild flowers are scattered on the hillside like living
confetti.

Something has happened to my body. It feels looser,
as though it has broken free and is floating.

I have been going to dream workshops at 7.00 a.m. The
facilitator is a nice American woman dream therapist called
Clara. I told her about a recurring dream I have that I am
trying to pick up the last pea on my dinner plate by stabbing
it with a fork. Try as I may, I cannot get the prongs of the
fork to stab into the flesh of the pea.

For years I have woken up feeling frustrated and hungry
after dreaming my pea dream.

Clara advised me to look at the dream from the *pea*'s
point of view. I did try hard to do this and, by discussing
it with Clara later, I understood that I, Adrian Mole, was
the pea and that the fork represented DEATH.

Clara said that my pea dream showed that I am afraid
to die.

But who is *looking forward* to death? I don't know anybody
who is cock-a-hoop at the prospect.

Clara explained that I am *morbidly* afraid of death.

How do you feel about death, Jo Jo?

I have made friends with the bloke with the beaded
plaits like yours. His name is Sean Washington. His mother
is Irish; his father is from St Kitts. He is here taking the
stress management course, but he hangs out with the
writers' group on the bar terrace.

We were both on vegetable chopping duties today and I
was complimented by him and others on my expertise. I
think I would like to be a chef. I may ask Savage if he'll
give me a trial when I get back.

Angela Hacker has forbidden her writers' group to use
clichés, but she will not be reading this letter, so I'll sign
off by saying:

> Wish you were here,
> Adrian

Saturday April 11th

My first fax! It was addressed to 'Adrian Mole, Faxos Institute', and arrived at the travel agent's shop in the town. It was then conveyed to the Faxos Institute by greengrocer's van and delivered to me on the bar terrace by Julian, the handsome bald-headed administrator. It caused a sensation.

> Dear Adrian,
> Thank you for your letters. I wish I were there with you. It sounds idyllic.
> I'm so glad that you feel at ease. When I first saw you in Savage's kitchen, I thought: that man is in *pain*. I wanted to touch you and comfort you there and then, but of course one does not do such a thing – not in England.
> I think you have it in your power to become a happy man, providing you can let go of the past. Why not try to live in the present and leave all that baggage behind on Faxos when you return?
> I couldn't wait to tell you that I have been offered a shared exhibition of 'Young Contemporaries' in September. Will you come to the opening? Please say you will.
> Roberto is complaining that the man Savage has hired to take your place for a fortnight is massacring the vegetables and he now regrets letting you go on holiday.
> Everybody at 'Savages' sends their best wishes. Roberto asks if you will bring a bottle of ouzo back for him.
> I miss you.
> I send you my best wishes as well,
> Jo Jo

Hut Number Six
Faxos Institute
Faxos
Sunday April 12th

Dear Jo Jo,

What fantastic news about the exhibition! Of course I will
come to the opening. September seems a long way off,
though. The spring is so glorious here. I've never seen
such colours before.

At our meeting yesterday morning Angela Hacker asked
the writers' group to write the first page of a novel.

I wanted to run up the hill to my hut immediately
and present her with the whole manuscript of *Lo! The Flat
Hills of My Homeland*, but I restrained myself. The book
was only a few pages short of completion. Why spoil the ship
for a ha'p'orth of tar? (Since being forbidden to use
clichés, I find myself using them all the time.)

I worked all day and most of the night on *Lo!* And
I think that now the book is finished. This is how it ends:

Jake got up from his computer terminal and paced
around his study. He adjusted the painting of a stately
African woman that he had recently bought in an exhibition.

He then stared moodily out of the window and
watched a child dragging a stick along the ground.

Jake was desperate to finish *Sparg from Kronk*. He
could hear the printer banging on his door, demand-
ing the finished manuscript. His publisher had been
admitted to hospital the night before with nervous
strain, but the ending of his book continued to elude
him.

The child outside the window stopped to scratch
the stick into the dry earth of drought-hit London.

'Goddit!' shouted Jake, and he leaped into his
state-of-the-art typing chair and began to write the
end of his book.

Sparg wrestled with Krun, his father, for possession
of the stick. He wondered why they were fighting over

this particular stick. There were plenty of others lying around.

He looked at his father's old face, now disfigured by anger, and thought: why are we *doing* this? He let go of the stick and allowed his father to take it away.

Sparg sat on the baked earth and thought, if only there was *language*, we wouldn't have to be so damned *physical*.

He poked his finger into the dust. He drew it along. In a few minutes, he had made marks and symbols.

Before the sun had gone down, he had written the first page of his novel. He hoped it wouldn't rain in the night and obliterate his work.

Tomorrow, he would continue his work inside a cave, he thought. What should he call his novel? He grunted to himself and tried out several titles. Finally, he settled on one and hurried to the big cave to scratch it on the wall before he forgot:

A BOOK WITH NO LANGUAGE

Yes, that was it. And he picked up a stick and began to gnaw the end of it into a point.

Jake could hardly wait for the electronic printer to spew out the typewritten page.

'At last,' he jubilated, 'I have finished *Sparg from Kronk*!'

Please let me know what you think, Jo Jo. I really value your opinion.

I gave the completed manuscript to Angela Hacker this morning. She took it from me and groaned, 'Sodding hell. I only asked for one page!' Then she put it into the blue raffia bag that she carries everywhere with her and continued her conversation with Clara about a dream she'd had of being chased by a giant cockroach.

At 11.00 p.m., after spending the evening with my friends, singing on the bar terrace, I got back to my hut to find that the following note had been slipped under my door:

Adrian,
I've skipped through *Lo! The Flat Hills of My Homeland*.
I won't waste words. It's typical juvenilia and has no
merit at all. *Sparg from Kronk* has been done a million
times, dearest boy. But *A Book With No Language* –
Sparg's novel – is a truly brilliant concept.

I would like you to come and see me when we get
back to London. I'd like to introduce you to my agent,
Sir Gordon Giles. I think your originality will appeal
to him.

Congratulations! You are a writer.
Angela Hacker

I may be a writer, Jo Jo, but I can't find the words
to express my happiness.

My plane gets into Gatwick on Wednesday at 3.00 p.m.
Love from,
Adrian

Tuesday   April 14th

Angela Hacker announced this morning that the writers'
group's last meeting was to be held on 'Bare Bum Beach'. My
penis shrivelled at the thought. I have never appeared in the
nude in public before. 'Bare Bum Beach' is where the extrovert
and confident desport themselves. I am neither of these things.
However, after three glasses of retsina at lunchtime I found
myself slithering over the rocks, heading for the nudist beach.

I was astounded by the ridiculous blue of the sea. The rocks
shone pink as I stumbled towards the beach which was the
colour of custard. It seemed the most natural thing in the world
to shrug my shorts off and embrace the sand. For twelve long
years I have worried about the size of my penis. Now, at last, by
glancing at my fellow male writers I could see that I am made
as other men. I easily fell within the 'normal' range.

At half past six in the evening I turned over and exposed
myself to the sun. Nothing terrible happened. There was no
thunderbolt. Men and women did not run away, shrieking in
horror at the sight of my full frontal nakedness.

I walked into the sea and swam towards the blood-red sunset. I allowed myself to float and to drift. It was almost dark when I swam back to the beach. I did not use my towel. I let the water dry on my body.

I walked back to the Institute in pale moonlight. I took a short cut through the woods. The floor was covered in pine needle debris, every footstep was a crackling aromatic delight.

I walked ankle deep through a glade of soft grass and wild flowers. Then I smelled honeysuckle and felt a tendril brush across my face. I reached the headland and stood for a moment, looking down at the Institute. The kitchen door was open. Out of it spilled bright light, laughter and the delicious smell of grilling meat.

Wednesday   April 15th

10.00 p.m. I saw Jo Jo waiting beyond the barrier. I threw all my baggage down and ran towards her.